PRAISE FOR
Joy's Summertime Adventures

Young girls desperately need reading materials that will encourage them to aspire to have a closer relationship with God. As children cross over from childhood to young adulthood, they need role models that will guide them in the right direction. Books can be a very powerful influence in the decisions that children make for adulthood. Anna has created a book that is authentic in the fun activities that children and their families engage in and still allow space for the heart to seek after God. She has developed a story that will draw in a young reader to enjoy the book as well as point her in a direction that will take her to a deeper relationship with God. Not only has she written a book about seeking after God, she exemplifies it in her life as well. Our children need materials that encourage them to seek after a relationship with God.

—**Joan Stowell,** Pastor's Wife, *Sahuarita First Assembly of God, Sahuarita, Arizona*

***

There is no better family than the Evans to teach the value of spirituality and the wisdom of keeping Christ at the center of our lives. Practical, relevant, and encouraging! I can't imagine a more practical book on a much-needed topic. Nor can I imagine a better person than Anna to write it. Finally, the perfect book written to help me prepare my children for a strong and solid spiritual future. I strongly urge every parent, and child, to read this book, apply these principles, and change their family's legacy and eternal security. Thank you, Anna, for this rock-solid guide to teach our kids and families the importance of keeping God first and Jesus Christ at the center as they grow into spiritually-mature adults with confidence and integrity.
—**Ahmad Alexander**, AuD, MPH, PMP, PHR, Licensed Minister, Retired Army, *Houston, Texas*

***

What a joy it was to read *Joy's Summertime Adventures*! Your storytelling captures the fun and wonder of childhood, and I'm sure your readers will love the adventures you've created. Writing a book is an incredible accomplishment, and your ability to bring joy and imagination to life through your words is inspiring. Keep dreaming, keep writing, and never stop sharing your stories with the world. I can't wait to see where your creativity takes you next!
—**Cheryl Sacks**, Author and Co-Founder, *BridgeBuilders Int'l, Phoenix, Arizona*

***

Joy's Summertime Adventures is a heartwarming and faith-filled story that follows Joy Snavely through a series of exciting summer experiences. From her elementary school graduation to adventures at summer camp and days spent with family and friends, each chapter reveals Joy's growing relationship with God. The book beautifully captures the simplicity and joy of childhood while weaving in important lessons about faith, friendship, and family. Readers will easily relate to Joy's everyday adventures, whether it's trying new activities, navigating friendships, or balancing fun with responsibility, all while being inspired by her desire to deepen her connection with God.

What makes Joy's Summertime Adventures especially relatable is how it reflects the familiar challenges and joys of growing up. Joy's experiences, whether learning the importance of obedience, stepping out of her comfort zone, or finding new ways to stay entertained, are situations young readers will recognize from their own lives. The book emphasizes that faith and fun can go hand in hand, making it not only an exciting summer read but also a meaningful journey of spiritual growth. Joy's adventures remind readers that even in the most ordinary moments, there are valuable lessons and opportunities to connect with God.

—**Colin Block**, Undergraduate Admissions Counselor, *Nelson University, Waxahachie, Texas*

***

Anna did an excellent job bringing the awe and marvel of childhood adventure to life in, *Joys Summertime Adventures!* I think many children can relate to the various escapades and sentiments that take place in the book. It is written in a warm, sweet, whimsical way that will take even the oldest of adults back in time to reminisce fondly about their own childhood summertime adventures.

—**Amber Polivchak**, President, *Christian Home Educators of Tucson, South East (CHET-SE), Tucson, Arizona*

***

It is such a delight being immersed into *Joy's Summertime Adventures.* There is something so sincerely heartwarming in the descriptions of each moment, character, and setting. As I read through this journey I couldn't help but pause and reflect on the ups and downs of my own childhood summertime adventures. God was always showing up, in the same way He does for Joy. This is a tale that will bring rest and gratitude to your soul.

—**Clayton Brooks,** Songwriter and Worship Pastor, *Calvary Church, Greensboro, North Carolina*

JOY'S SUMMERTIME ADVENTURES

ANNA EVANS

Published by KHARIS PUBLISHING, an imprint of
KHARIS MEDIA LLC.

Copyright © 2025 Anna Evans

ISBN-13: 978-1-63746-309-3
ISBN-10: 1-63746-309-X
Library of Congress Control Number: 2024951042

Illustrations by Anna Evans

All KHARIS PUBLISHING products are available at
special quantity discounts for bulk purchase for sales
promotions, premiums, fund-raising, and educational
needs. For details, contact:
Kharis Media LLC
Tel: 1-630-909-3405
support@kharispublishing.com
www.kharispublishing.com

CONTENTS

Chapter 1

GRADUATION

"What's taking Mommy and Daddy so long to come downstairs?" Joy mused. She huffed impatiently and plopped down on the brick-red paisley living room recliner. While waiting, Joy Snavely reflected on her life.

Her parents were Mr. and Mrs. Snavely, but Joy and her brother Ethan called them Mommy and Daddy. Joy loved and respected her parents; she knew they loved her, too.

Mommy was kind and gentle with her children, but she made sure they did their chores and behaved themselves. Mommy worked daily: she cooked delicious meals, kept the house tidy, paid bills, and ran errands. She also helped Joy and Ethan with their homework.

Interestingly, Mommy was Hispanic. Her background brought exotic foods to the table (such as passionfruit and plantains), and she encouraged the children to speak Spanish. Ethan and Joy could speak the foreign language reasonably well, yet there were still some rough spots. In fact, there were times when "Spanglish" was necessary to get the point across.

On the other hand, Daddy was American. Although he did not speak Spanish, Daddy knew some German. He was a platoon sergeant in the Army. The Snavely Family usually moved every one to three years because of his career. Currently, he was stationed at Ft. Hood, Texas. Daddy liked to make jokes and play video games with Joy and Ethan.

Most days, Daddy held devotions with his family, similar to Bible studies. He would read a passage from the Bible, which was brought to him by the Holy Spirit, and ask the children questions about the Scripture.

Daddy also dug deeper into well-known Bible stories and explained them in such a way they seemed tied together by Jesus. Daddy said, "He is the scarlet cord that is woven throughout the Word." Sometimes, Daddy's teachings made Joy realize how wonderfully real God was in her life, even more real than the air she breathed.

Joy was ten years old. Her brother Ethan was eight, two years younger than Joy. Ethan liked to tease Joy, and Joy could be a little short-tempered with him when she was annoyed, but they really loved each other and had fun playing together. It was a classic brother-and-sister relationship.

Ethan liked cars, planes, and trains. His hobby was building models of cars and airplanes. His favorite animals were dinosaurs, and Mommy had decorated his room with them. Ethan's favorite color was dark green, which he used as the main color scheme in his room.

Graduation

Joy's thoughts wandered to her bedroom. Dolly, Joy's doll and companion since Joy's preschool days, rested against the pillows in her bedroom. Dolly was a sweet rag doll, and Joy still slept with her. Dolly's McIntosh-apple-shaped face was adorned with jet-black, shoe-button eyes, and a mouth sewn with red thread. Her chestnut-colored yarn hair was gathered into two ponytails. Dolly wore a tan dress decorated with cloth flowers and little grey shoes on her feet.

Mommy had kept Dolly in excellent condition, so she looked almost new. *"Mommy told me that when I was younger, I used to carry Dolly everywhere,"* Joy smiled reflectively. Along with Dolly, Joy had an array of stuffed animals, which were her favorite toys. Enormous elephants, bears, and other creatures lined the top rack of Joy's closet.

Joy's hobbies were reading and doing projects such as putting jigsaw puzzles together. Her favorite animal had always been the elephant; however, now she was drawn toward horses.

Joy's family lived twenty minutes from Ft. Hood in a town called Belton. Their home was located in a growing neighborhood close to Stillhouse Hollow Lake. There were hiking trails in the neighborhood, and one trail led to the Lampasas River. The river attracted the family to the community.

"Click-clack, click-clack." The rapid sound of Skippy's nails hitting the tile floor interrupted Joy's train of thought. Skippy, a Miniature Schnauzer and the Snavely family dog for a year now, trotted up to Joy and wagged his short tail.

Skippy was black with white markings on his throat, chest, and three of his paws. Joy cuddled him whenever she could and gave him countless silly names. Skippy knew several tricks, and Joy was teaching him more.

However, Skippy had some faults. He barked at other people and sometimes ran out into the street. Also, he retaliated by biting when caught stealing things.

Joy and her best friend, Elizabeth Teller, had just finished fifth grade the day before, and Ethan completed fourth grade. They were homeschooled through the Christian A Beka Accredited Program. Later that evening, the Snavely and Teller families would celebrate Joy and Elizabeth's graduation from elementary to middle school. They would also honor Ethan.

Ethan suddenly appeared atop the stairs, then jumped onto the banister and slid down the rest of the way.

"Ethan, didn't Mommy tell us not to slide down the railing in our good clothes?" Joy asked. Ethan simply grinned at his sister and went to the kitchen.

Joy stared at the large clock on the wall. (*"It's 4:26 p.m., and Elizabeth and her family are supposed to arrive at 4:30 p.m. I hope they aren't late."*)

Joy had met Elizabeth, also ten years old, in church the first week that Joy and her family arrived in Texas. Elizabeth had a four-year-old sister and a 15-month-old baby brother. Elizabeth kept a pet rabbit in her room, and her family had two cats.

Joy rose from her chair and went into the formal dining room just off the foyer. Joy always enjoyed this room. A long, mahogany table sat in the center of the room, bordered by six chairs. Two unused dining chairs framed the window, with a small, round table between them. Antique lamps, candleholders, and paintings were all around the dining room, and a gold-edged mirror rested on a marble-topped armoire.

Joy noticed a couple of lamp cables were showing under the furniture, so she bent down to reroute them. As she did so, Joy heard Mommy and Daddy coming downstairs. In her excitement to greet them, Joy bumped her mortarboard off her head.

"Mommy, can you please fix my hat? It's hard to put it back on."

Mommy smiled and arranged Joy's hat. Ethan appeared from the kitchen with a yogurt cup in his hand.

"Finish that up and brush your teeth," Mommy insisted. "I don't want our guests seeing you with that!"

Daddy was sitting in the foyer, checking his cell phone. Joy approached him and gave him a hug. Then, Daddy motioned for Joy to have snuggle time with him. Snuggle time was one of Joy's favorite parts of her relationship with Daddy. She sat down on his lap and threw her arms around his neck. Joy remained with Daddy for at least five minutes, soaking up his love. She sighed happily and closed her eyes. There was no need for words.

Before long, Mommy called Joy to help her with the snacks for the graduation party. Mommy arranged a platter of fruit, which included apples, berries, kiwis, and grapes. Joy dumped a bag of tortilla chips into one of Mommy's big bowls and dished out the salsa. She watched as Mommy set out the homemade flyers announcing the night's events. It read as follows: "Graduation Ceremony: (1) Report Card Presentation, (2) Handing Out of Honor Rolls, (3) Picture Session, (4) Snacks, (5) Presents, (6) Games, and (7) Eating Out."

After a while, a car rolled up the street and stopped in front of the Snavely house. When the doorbell rang, Skippy charged out of nowhere and began barking ferociously. The Tellers had arrived!

Amid all the commotion, Joy got Elizabeth's attention and began chatting with her. Both girls were wearing their graduation gowns and could hardly wait to begin the ceremony.

Mommy invited everyone into the living room for the graduation ceremony, which she would show on screen. She had made a display on the television of the children's report cards. It took a couple of minutes to actually initiate the presentation since Ashton and Kimberly, Elizabeth's younger siblings, kept fussing.

First, Mommy asked Daddy to lead everyone in prayer. He began by thanking God for the great effort the children had made, knowing they had done it for Him and not for people. The children were blessed to learn in a Christian environment at home, and even when school was out, they could learn godly principles and ways to grow in their walk with God. Next, the report card presentation began.

After the presentation, Daddy gave Joy and Ethan their honor roll certificates, and Mr. Teller handed Elizabeth her honor roll certificate. All the while, Joy noticed Mommy and Mrs. Teller taping them with their camcorders. Joy soon got tired of smiling so much for two cameras at once. She knew that Ethan and Elizabeth felt the same way.

All three children were excited to open their gifts. Joy received a Pom-Pom Puppy craft project and a big jigsaw puzzle from the Tellers. Mommy and Daddy gave her the *Little House on the Prairie* book collection.

Joy thanked the Tellers and her parents for the gifts. She showed Elizabeth and Ethan her things, and Skippy came to sniff, also.

"Careful, Skippy," warned Joy when he was getting too nosy.

Then Ethan showed Joy his gifts. Joy studied Ethan's cool plane model set and new board game, *Chutes and Ladders*.

Mommy carried a stack of board games into the living room. Everyone joined in to play several rounds of *Scattergories*, *Uno*, and *Chutes and Ladders*.

When they were done playing, it was time to leave for dinner at Italian Garden. When they arrived at the restaurant, the Snavelys and Tellers sat down at a large table and waited for their meal. Mommy took a photo of Joy, Elizabeth, and Ethan sitting together, and then both families said grace.

For dessert, the waiters came out with slices of rich chocolate cake, tiramisu, and strawberry cheesecake. After a few bites, Joy's chocolate cake tasted too sweet, so she pushed her plate Ethan's way, who gladly finished it off for her. Joy frowned disapprovingly at her brother as he crammed cake into his mouth and left a mess on his face.

Finally, the Snavelys and Tellers said their goodbyes. When the Snavelys got home, it was time for Joy and Ethan to get ready for bed. Before climbing into bed, Joy pulled out her Bible.

Opening randomly, she found herself at Luke 21:38, where it said the people got up early in the morning to hear Jesus speak. Joy pondered the sentence for a minute. (*"That sounds like something I should do: get up early in the morning to read my Bible."*)

Joy snuggled under her covers and breathed a sigh of fulfillment. "Dear God, I'm so glad that summer vacation is finally here!"

Chapter 2

FIRST DAYS OF VACATION

The sunlight was fairly bursting into Joy's room as she woke up. Joy threw back her covers, slipped into her flip-flops, went to the window, and twisted the blinds open. (*Wow! It's beautiful outside: the sky is so clear and blue. It's certainly a Sunday…Wait! Are those birds singing?*) Joy opened her window. She pressed her face against the screen to breathe in the fresh air, only…it didn't smell so fresh. "Blah!" Joy exclaimed as she smelled the dust and pollen trapped on the screen.

Joy waited awhile before closing her window so she could listen to the birds sing. She strained to hear the faint but sweet and heavenly notes of an oriole. The oriole's song reminded her of sparkling dew dripping off grass on a cool, still sunrise.

Removing herself from her reverie, Joy turned around to complete her morning routine. When Joy sat down to read her Bible, she flipped over to Philippians, the Book of Joy, and read chapter 4. Philippians 4 had many key verses on living a godly life.

When Joy came downstairs, she found that Daddy would be home all day, since it was both a Sunday and Mother's Day.

Right now, Daddy was sitting in his place at the dining room table, leafing through his Bible and old, battered concordance. Daddy had had this same concordance while he studied biblical theology in college. Joy guessed Daddy was preparing his devotional message for the day.

"Good morning, Daddy! Happy Mother's Day, Mommy!" Joy shouted. Mommy was in the kitchen, cooking a great-smelling breakfast. A loud thudding resounding from the staircase announced Ethan's arrival. "Hi, Ethan!" Joy greeted her brother.

Suddenly, Mommy called from the kitchen, "Joy, can you feed the dog?" Joy came up and giggled as she watched Skippy jump up on his hind legs, "dance" in front of Mommy, and make little grunting noises—his way of asking for food. "Come on, Skippy," Joy cried, as she excused herself to feed Skippy. As usual, Skippy wolfed down his food with gusto! Joy washed her hands and set the table.

When breakfast ended, everyone went back upstairs to get ready for church. Joy put on a soft summer dress Mommy had laid out for her and a pearl bead necklace. Next, Joy brushed her teeth and asked Mommy to fix her hair.

On the way to church, Joy sat carefully to avoid wrinkling her clothes or soil her new cloth shoes. She gazed out the window at the fluffy white clouds and green stands of trees.

After parking in their usual spot at church, Joy and her family walked into the cool building and took their places in the sanctuary. Occasionally, Joy and Ethan went to children's church, but most of the time they stayed with their parents in the main service.

After the seats had mostly filled, the doors were closed, and Pastor Kearney announced upcoming events on the church's calendar. Then the worship team led the congregation in hymns and songs of praise. Afterwards, Pastor Kearney began his sermon on Christian conduct toward one another.

Joy had a hard time focusing on Pastor's sermon. It was so easy to start looking up at the ceiling, or around at other people, or even down at patterns in the carpet and seats…but no. As she hid a yawn, Joy shook her head. (*"Jesus, help me to pay attention. I know I need to make every thought obedient to You. Help me to listen closely and put my mind on You."*) After praying, Joy found it easier to repel distraction and pay attention to Pastor Kearney's lesson.

After his sermon, Pastor Kearney closed the service with prayer, and the congregation was dismissed.

On the way home, Daddy stopped at a local supermarket so he, Joy, and Ethan could buy some presents for Mommy. Later, at home, they presented Mommy with their gifts. Together, Joy and Ethan gave Mommy a gift card to one of her favorite department stores and a signed birthday card. Daddy handed her a gorgeous bouquet of a dozen white roses tinged with pink and purple shades. Mommy thanked them all for their lovely gifts and immediately set her flowers in a vase beside Joy and Ethan's card.

Devotion in the afternoon was partly over the sermon at church and partly from Daddy's previous Bible research. Joy was glad she remembered the sermon and could answer most of Daddy's discussion questions concerning the true behavior of God's people. Then, Daddy taught on Christ's view of his church—all believers as a whole.

When devotion ended, Mommy began making dinner. She made some delicious spaghetti using her special recipe. Joy helped Mommy prepare the meal by stirring the simmering pasta, baking the garlic cheese toast, and setting the table. The family sat down to enjoy their spaghetti, and Daddy and Ethan added mountains of Parmesan cheese to their pasta before digging in!

After dinner, Mommy asked Daddy and Ethan to bring out suitcases from the garage, and she packed clothes, hygiene items, shoes, and towels. Joy was mystified when Mommy did not explain.

Around 8:00 p.m., Joy went to bed and slept until the alarm clock on her nightstand rang unexpectedly. Joy placed her hand over the two bells to muffle the clapper; this trick minimized the piercing ring while Joy groped for the "OFF" button. Since it was still dark outside, Joy wanted to see the time. As she switched on the clock's light, she gasped, "What! It's 4:00 a.m." As Joy put her clock back in its place, she spotted a light shining under her bedroom door. Curiosity overcame her sleepiness: Joy crept softly out of bed and opened the door cautiously. (*"Huh, what's going on?"*)

Mommy, coming out of the master bedroom, saw Joy and told her to shower and get ready.

"What's going on, Mommy?" Joy asked drowsily. She shivered and wished to be back in her warm bed.

"We're leaving on a trip," Mommy answered briefly. Mommy might have said more to Joy, but at that moment Daddy called Mommy from the master bedroom.

"But where are we going?" Joy inquired again, but Mommy had already closed her door. Joy shrugged and sat down in the nearest chair to wait for her brother, who was already in the shower. Joy nearly fell asleep by the time the bathroom door lock turned and Ethan came out.

"Boy, you look tired," remarked Ethan. Joy playfully stuck her tongue out at him and then disappeared into the bathroom. After a cold rinse to wake her up, Joy got dressed. All the while, Joy yawned until her jaw ached. Joy went downstairs with her packed suitcase and bookbag. Her bag was full of enough books and word puzzles to last two trips!

When Joy said, "Good morning, boy!" Skippy got up and stretched himself like a cat. Since the family was taking Skippy on their road trip, Joy packed dog food, chew bones, and treats in a black duffle bag. She also stuffed a blanket and harness into the bag.

It took a few minutes to gather everyone's belongings and get organized, but the family was finally ready. After closing up their house, Joy and her family filed outside and stepped into Mommy's SUV, which Daddy had thoughtfully warmed beforehand. Daddy stacked the suitcases in the trunk, and off they drove!

Outside the car, it was completely dark, except where streetlamps cast a circle of golden, glowing light. "Where can we be going?" Joy wondered, but less inquisitively since she had first asked the question. Sleepiness had crept back into Joy as excitement and anticipation wore off. Joy twisted in her seat to find a comfortable position. Joy took off her shoes and curled up. She used Skippy's furry back as a pillow and closed her eyes to sleep.

Joy awakened around 6:30 a.m. to a rather overcast sunrise. Her arm was "asleep" from lying on it. Joy peeked over at her brother, sleeping soundly and hugging his Teddy Bear.

First Days of Vacation

Teddy was a small, blue bear, with a cuddly look on his face. He was extremely floppy; he couldn't even sit up. His head was stuffed with cotton filling, but his middle had hard little beads in it. Whenever Joy teased Ethan, Teddy would be Ethan's "secret weapon" to drive Joy away. Those hard beads stung when Joy received a "Teddy-smack."

"*Hola, muñeca mia* (Good morning, Darling)," Mommy said, seeing Joy was awake.

Joy replied sleepily, "Hi, Mommy. Where are we?"

"Close to Dallas," Mommy answered. "We will stop for breakfast, so put your shoes back on and wake up your brother."

Joy called Ethan to wake him. Ethan blinked his eyes and yawned. "Are we there yet?" he asked.

"No, not really," Joy replied. "We're going to have breakfast first."

The family chose to eat breakfast at Pancake House. Daddy rolled down the windows a bit so Skippy could have cool, fresh air. Skippy whined plaintively when he saw his family leaving, but he couldn't enter the restaurant. Skippy's whimpers faded as the family entered the building.

Joy's family chose a booth near a window to keep an eye on Skippy. They talked and laughed together as they ate.

Back outside after breakfast, Joy saw a group of sparrows feeding nearby. "Here you go," Joy told the sparrows, holding out a leftover pancake. She threw pancake pieces on the ground, and the sparrows pecked at the bits and flew away with them.

The family returned to the car and tried to calm Skippy, who was in a frenzy. Joy scooped some food for Skippy and set it in his travel dish.

As a rule, whenever Daddy stopped during a road trip (for instance, at a restaurant), he went to the nearest gas station and refueled the car. No one is ever sure of a fuel station farther up the road, and Daddy wasn't taking any chances on running out of gas and becoming stranded. Previous experience had taught Daddy that.

While the tank filled, Daddy asked, "Got any trash?" Joy and Ethan donated some gum wrappers, empty water bottles, and balled-up facial tissue.

Since the family didn't have devotion before leaving on their trip, Mommy played an audio devotional on her phone. After hearing the devotional, Joy and Ethan prayed, thanking God for the new day and safety on the remainder of the trip.

When prayer was over, Joy and Ethan occupied their time by working on dot-to-dot books. Skippy settled down on his blanket and gnawed his treat bone.

Another hour passed, and Joy asked, "How much longer until we get there?"

"Just about one more hour," Mommy replied.

Joy sighed. She did not want to color or connect dots anymore. Apparently, neither did Ethan. Instead, Daddy began to tell them stories. He had a wonderful ability to tell stories—whether real or made-up—so that, no matter how often he told one, each story was exciting to hear. Joy remembered, when she and Ethan were younger, their favorite story had been "The Three Little Pigs." They had begged Daddy to tell it every single night.

About forty-five minutes later, Daddy turned onto Ranch Parkway. Daddy's parents lived on this road. *("So that's what Mommy and Daddy planned for our first activity of the summer: a visit with Grandmama and Grandaddy!")*

The family's SUV rumbled along a gravel driveway leading to a tidy farmhouse. Joy craned her neck to look out the back window and watch the tan, billowing clouds of dust behind them. Joy's attention was caught by movement along the side of the driveway. When she realized what it was, she motioned Ethan to look and exclaimed, "Look! Those are chickens scratching. There! Behind that wire fence."

Somehow, Skippy could tell the trip had ended. He whined and stood on Joy's stomach to look out the window. "Ouch!" cried Joy.

The car rolled to a stop. As if on cue, Grandmama and Grandaddy walked out of the house. A beagle raced in front of them and barked. At a word from Grandaddy, however, the dog stopped and sat down.

Joy jumped down from the car and hugged her grandparents. "Come on inside," Grandmama said.

Chapter 3

STAY AT GRANDMAMA AND GRANDADDY'S HOUSE

Grandmama showed the family a guest room where they could stay. Joy and Ethan set their bags in separate corners of the room. Skippy and the beagle, Sparks, settled down and became friends.

The family settled into chairs in the living room and talked until Grandmama excused herself from the conversation and got up to finish dinner. Mommy and Joy went to help her with the little bit of cooking that was left. Meanwhile, Daddy and Grandaddy continued talking, and Ethan played with his new model plane set on the kitchen counter.

On the floor, Skippy and Sparks hunted around for dropped food. Joy occasionally gave them a kernel of corn or a section of blackberry but tried not to feed them too much.

When the food was served, everyone drew chairs to the table. As she sat down, Joy noted the style of the table. It was of a very dark wood and had a scrolled design carved on its sides and legs. Clearly, it was antique; the table was very old, yet very beautiful.

While Joy ate, she realized Grandmama was a great cook. Her chili was flavorful and rich, yet not too spicy. Her recipe for dinner rolls was foolproof. The rolls were delightfully crusty on the outside, yet soft and melt-in-your-mouth inside. Grandmama's last treat of the meal, blackberry cobbler, was just the right balance between sweetness and lightness. Joy wished she could cook like Grandmama.

At the end of the meal, everyone went to the living room where they could talk some more. Joy and Ethan kept their ears open to the adult's conversation. By now, the overcast skies had turned to rain and there was a faint rumble of thunder in the distance.

When the old clock on the fireplace mantel struck eight gongs, Joy and Ethan prepared for bed. Grandmama gave Mommy blankets and sheets to make Joy's and Ethan's beds on the floor. In a few minutes, Joy lay down between the cool sheets in her makeshift bed with Skippy at her side. Joy whispered goodnight to her brother and rolled over.

Joy listened to the comforting patter of raindrops and the now-louder rolls of thunder. Joy pulled the covers up tighter when she saw a flash of lightning. (*"Dear Lord, thank you for the rain, the lightning, and the thunder. Thank you for letting us make it safely to Grandmama and Grandaddy's house. I pray we'll have a great day tomorrow. In Jesus' name, amen.")*

The next morning, Joy woke up to find Mommy and Daddy gone. Since Ethan was still snoozing, Joy crept out of her bed softly so she wouldn't wake her brother.

Twenty minutes later, Joy went to the sunny kitchen where Grandmama was making breakfast.

"Good morning," said Grandmama, "Did you sleep well last night?"

"Yes, ma'am," replied Joy, "Do you know where Mommy and Daddy are?"

"They're both outside… And please tell them that breakfast is almost ready," said Grandmama. Joy skipped outside to find Mommy sitting on the porch.

Joy spotted Daddy and Grandaddy strolling around the yard. "Good morning, Daddy. Good morning, Grandaddy," Joy said. "Grandmama says breakfast is almost ready."

Inside, everyone, including a sleepy-eyed Ethan, washed up for breakfast. Grandmama had made spinach-tomato omelet wedges and sourdough biscuits slathered with gravy. The family asked God to bless the food, then passed around the plates.

After eating, Joy helped Mommy and Grandmama wash the dishes. Before long, Joy invented a new game with Skippy: she jiggled the soap bottle, quickly opened the cap, and squeezed the bottle gently. Bubbles filled the air, and Skippy and even Sparks tried to eat them.

After the kitchen was clean, the family sat down in the living room to have devotion. Grandaddy led the devotion; he spoke on faith. Grandaddy gave small starters of several Bible verses such as Hebrews 11:6 so Joy and Ethan could quote them. They only needed help with a few verses.

After devotion closed with prayer, Grandaddy went to the garage and brought out a croquet set. He and Daddy erected the posts and wickets and showed Mommy, Joy, and Ethan how to play the game.

When Joy's turn came, she set her heavy red ball on the ground and gave it a sharp tap with her mallet. The wooden ball rolled to a stop in the general direction of the next wicket. Then, it was Ethan's turn.

"Croquet's fun," Joy thought and said so aloud. It was pretty challenging, though, as uneven ground and a miscalculated hit could send the ball far off course. Although she lost, Joy asked excitedly if the family could play another round.

As they were playing, Joy kept glancing at Grandmama and Grandaddy's pool, which was adjacent to the area where they played croquet. When Joy least expected it, Grandaddy asked if Joy and her brother would like to play in the pool. They exclaimed with excitement, "Yes!" and ran off to get some pool things.

Joy set a beach towel on a lawn chair to warm in the sun. She looked at the shimmering blue oblong of water in the pool. It had a diving board over the deeper end and a pleasant waterfall that tumbled over rocks into the pool.

Grandaddy was heating up the grill on the patio so Grandmama and Mommy could cook hamburgers and hotdogs. Joy and Ethan came outside and saw the cooks fighting the pesky flies attempting to land on the food. Skippy snapped at the low-flying ones. Mommy made a disgusted sound when she saw Skippy smacking on a fly. "Eww!" Joy exclaimed. Even *she* thought it was gross. Ethan laughed.

Before Joy and Ethan jumped into the pool, Mommy called, "Come have lunch!" Joy forgot she would have to wait half an hour before getting into the pool if she ate.

Joy and Ethan had just finished eating a hamburger, a hotdog, salad, chips with salsa, and vanilla ice cream and were about to enter the pool when Mommy said, "Ethan! Joy!"

Mommy's calling them reminded Joy that they had to wait before getting into the pool. Joy groaned in disappointment, but she knew it was good advice. Joy remembered one time when she did not wait and had gotten cramps.

To pass the time, Joy wandered around the yard hunting for interesting objects. Here is what she found: a piece of a robin's egg, a small artificial geode, one of Grandmama's big sewing needles, and a large maple leaf.

Cicadas hummed in the trees and grasshoppers buzzed in the lawn. Joy caught a few grasshoppers and released them after studying them closely. Then Ethan came up, with a huge smile on his face and his hands clasped together. "What did you catch?" Joy asked. Ethan shoved his hands in front of Joy's face and opened them. Joy shrieked when she saw a toad inches from her face. Joy normally didn't mind creatures like toads, but she shivered at the idea of one jumping on her when it was that close. "Where did you find him?" Joy asked after getting over her shock.

"I found him next to the AC units, by the garage," Ethan replied. Joy smiled as she watched her brother play with his new pet in the grass. Ethan named him Toady. So he wouldn't lose Toady while swimming, Ethan asked the adults for a place to keep his pet. Grandaddy gave him a big plastic bucket. Ethan sprayed a little water into it from the hose, then added stones, grass, and twigs. He gently set Toady in the water and entrusted the toad to Mommy's care.

Meanwhile, Joy went to visit Grandmama's hens. She opened the small gate of the wire chicken pen and made sure to shut the gate again so the dogs wouldn't get in and agitate the chickens. Joy had read in one of her books that if chickens are startled enough, they won't lay eggs for weeks! She avoided making sudden movements. Joy squatted down and petted the nearest hen. She watched the chickens as they ate, drank, and pecked at new objects, including Joy's finger!

Stay at Grandmamu and Gradaddys House

Next, Joy wandered around Grandaddy's three-acre land. It was a small farm consisting of chickens, a vegetable garden, and a shed housing Grandaddy's big, red, tractor-mower.

When thirty minutes were over, Joy ran to the pool with Skippy barking excitedly at her heels. Just before entering the pool, Joy stopped to kick off her flip-flops by her lawn chair. Ethan streaked past her and jumped into the pool, making a huge splash.

Grandaddy threw in some floats and a remote-controlled boat. When Ethan saw the boat, his face lit up. He grabbed Toady from the bucket and put the toad in the boat to send him spinning!

Toady abruptly leaped out of the boat and kicked to the nearest wall, but he couldn't scale the concrete. Ethan quickly grabbed Toady before the dogs ate him.

"Joy, can you go under and blow bubbles at Toady while he swims over you? I want to see what he does," Ethan asked. Joy dove close to the bottom of the pool. She rotated over on her back to look up and saw the swiftly moving underside of Toady. As she got closer, Joy blew a jet of bubbles at him. Then Joy rose to the surface for air. Ethan was staring at her head. "Look on your head!" he laughed.

At that moment, Joy felt something in her hair. She touched the top of her head and screamed. (*"What is this big, slimy thing?"*) She dove underwater quickly again to rid herself of the object on her head. It worked. "W-w-what was that?" Joy demanded when she rose to the surface, spluttering and choking.

Ethan explained. "That was Toady. He was bobbing on the bubbles you made and ended up right over your head." Joy smiled at Ethan's laughter in spite of herself.

While the adults looked on from the porch, Joy and Ethan raced each other, talked underwater, and jumped from the diving board, making greater and greater splashes.

After two hours of swimming and playing, Joy and Ethan waded out of the pool exhausted! Joy's teeth chattered as she rushed inside the cool house with a towel, trying not to leave water tracks everywhere.

After she had rinsed the pool water off herself, Joy went outside to help Ethan pick up the pool toys. Joy used a long net to scoop things out; meanwhile,

Ethan scurried to Toady's bucket to check on him. His face fell. "Toady looks sad," Ethan said soberly. He gently put Toady into his palm and dumped the contents of the bucket into the grass. Ethan turned his steps toward the AC units and set the toad where he had been found. "Bye, Toady," Ethan murmured, as he watched Toady disappear into the tall, feathery grass.

Joy saw Ethan's act of kindness. She came to Ethan and put her arm around him. "I think you did the right thing by putting Toady back," Joy reassured him. Ethan gave a sigh and said resignedly, "Oh well, I hope he lives *hop*-ily ever after." Joy laughed at Ethan's pun. Joy and her brother entered the house, and the memory of Toady slowly faded.

"Why don't we take a walk?" Grandmama was suggesting as Joy and Ethan came in. Joy immediately hooked on Skippy's leash, and everyone went out.

Sparks kept up calmly with the family without a leash. On the other hand, Skippy tugged on his leash and nearly pulled Joy to the ground. Before long, Ethan took over and held Skippy. Skippy wanted to sniff everything.

Grandmama and Grandaddy's house was built on the outskirts of an established neighborhood. While touring the neighborhood, Joy spotted a playground. She and Ethan sprinted ahead toward it, and Skippy and Sparks loped alongside.

Some children were on the playground, and Joy and Ethan played freeze tag with them. After the other children left, Joy tried crossing the monkey bars. Joy made it one-fourth of the way and then gave up. Ethan swung from one end to the other with ease.

Joy tried to prove herself by traversing the monkey bars again. She only made it to the second bar before her arms went limp. Joy let go and decided to try another day.

As the family continued walking, they came to a pond. There were ducks, geese, and even a heron. Ethan found some old dog biscuits in his pocket. He shared them with Joy so they could both feed the birds. The birds crowded around Joy; they seemed to like the treats. Mommy took a video of Joy and Ethan feeding the ducks and geese. She even filmed Joy nearly being pecked by a protective gander!

It happened this way: Joy tried to feed a mother goose and her goslings. Joy kept getting nearer and nearer until a gander charged her from nowhere. Joy turned to see the angry gander, yelled, and ran as fast as she possibly could to her family. If that gander had been two inches closer, he would have nipped Joy. In the safety of her parents, Joy scowled at Ethan, who was snickering over Joy's mishap.

As twilight fell, the family returned to the house. Every once in a while, Joy looked over her shoulder to see if the gander had followed her. At the house, the family, even Joy, had another good laugh over the video of the incident.

Chapter 4

Rodeo Surprise

"Ohh," groaned Joy the next morning when she awoke. Her limbs were decidedly sore from yesterday's exercise in the pool and at the playground. "Get ready, Joy; we're going somewhere today," Mommy called from where she was making the guest bed. "Ethan, wake up, *hijo*."

Breakfast was hot oatmeal with fruit and yogurt. After breakfast, Joy gave Skippy his dog food.

Daddy warmed the car. When the entire family was outside, Grandaddy took out a key from his pocket and locked the front door. Joy rode with her parents in the SUV, while Grandaddy took Grandmama and Ethan in his car. They agreed Daddy would go behind Grandaddy the entire trip. Joy watched as Grandaddy pulled out first. (*Well, here we go.*)

After one hour of driving, Joy and her family arrived at a rodeo ground. Joy squealed with delight when she saw they were going to a rodeo. "Thank you *sooo* much, Mommy and Daddy!" she exclaimed. As Joy later found out, Daddy had purchased discounted tickets to the rodeo at Fort Hood.

Around the outside of the rodeo stands was a crude parking lot. It was just a small field of grass marked by bright orange cones and spray-painted lines. The two separate parties of the Snavely family found parking spaces, linked up, and walked past rows of cars to the entrance. After validating their tickets and receiving a program, the family passed under the echoing stand and went up the clanging stairs to mid-level.

Joy gazed at her surroundings. The rodeo arena was similar to a football field (with the customary uncomfortable metal bleachers), but there was a maze of rusted metal fences, gates, and stalls on one side of the dirt field. A lookout tower, where Joy assumed the announcer was posted, stood near the cattle chutes.

Thankfully, Mommy had brought beach blankets and towels to sit on. The bleachers were hard, and Joy and Ethan were grateful when Mommy handed them each a neatly folded blanket.

As a soldier, Daddy always arrived early at events or appointments. Consequently, it would be more than thirty minutes before the rodeo commenced. To pass the time, Mommy took the children down to the concession booths.

At a food booth, Mommy bought two bags of praline pecans for Joy and Ethan. They soon came to the booth of a well-known insurance company; little stuffed animals in the shape of lizards were being given out to passersby. Joy and her brother asked for two stuffed animals.

Joy cuddled her new little toy and named it Geckie. Ethan called his lizard Spiny. To differentiate between Spiny and Geckie, Joy and Ethan looked at the shape of the features. One of Spiny's eyes protruded farther than the other, and Geckie's mouth was slightly crooked on one side.

Apparently, thirty minutes passed very quickly: the announcer began hollering something on the loudspeakers that Joy could not decipher. The rodeo was beginning, and Joy and Ethan pleaded with Mommy to get them back to the stands quickly. As soon as she saw the rest of the family, Joy raced ahead to take her seat.

Joy searched until she saw, coming out of the holding stalls on the far end of the field, the first saddle bronc rider. He was on a strawberry roan horse, who was bucking and kicking like a great whirlwind. Joy thought the rider would get whiplash by the way he was jerked about.

Many other people competed in the saddle bronc riding. Then there came calf roping. One by one, startled calves raced out of the chute and sturdy mounts chased them down. Lassos, which had been whipping around riders' heads, flew out flawlessly toward their catches. As both calves and horses stopped, riders jumped off, flipped calves over, and tied three of their legs.

During the calf roping, Joy had been secretly hoping that the rough treatment wasn't going to hurt the little calves. Now, she hoped the grown-up version of the calves—the steers—weren't going to hurt the riders! Rider after rider got tossed off madly fighting steers.

Soon half-time came, where everyone could go down to ground level and stretch their legs. By this time, Joy and her family had eaten all the praline pecans, and Joy wanted to get some lemonade, which was sold at a stand nearby. Joy sipped on it, but the sour-sweet, puckery lemonade made her want something salty. For that, nachos came to the rescue. Joy crunched on tortilla chips and tried not to splatter gooey cheese.

There was also entertainment for children during half-time. Joy was especially interested in riding a steer—though it was not a real one. The "steer," controlled by a joystick, was definitely less wild than the ones that Joy had seen in the arena. The catch, however, was the steer had nothing to hang on to. There was a kind of saddle, but it was more like a flat pad without a pommel, horn, stirrups…anything!

Joy got in line behind Ethan and watched as he fell after making a valiant effort to stay on the steer's back. Then it was Joy's turn. She straddled the steer and kept the balance as it swayed and rocked under her. Joy dug her fingernails into a gap under the "saddle" and held on. Finally, Joy began to slip. A couple of more clever moves on the part of the operator, and Joy fell down.

After halftime, there were barrel races, in which athletic horses raced in a specific pattern around three barrels. It was incredible the way competing horses rounded such sharp turns at nearly full speed!

Next were the rodeo clowns. They were similar to circus clowns, but they seriously saved cowboys' lives. The clowns rolled into the center of the field in a little ambulance. They came pouring out of the vehicle and performed stunts and silly tricks. When they finished, the rodeo clowns piled into the car and drove back to the exit gate, with car parts falling off everywhere. People all around Joy were chuckling. Joy and Ethan could hardly stop laughing. "That last trick was funny!" Joy remarked, giggling.

The rodeo continued with steer wrestling, breakaway roping, bareback riding, team roping, and bull riding.

The announcer listed the winners for the championship rounds of all the events, and awards were distributed. The indistinct PA system made it nearly impossible for Joy to hear what was said, so she kept asking Daddy questions about who won each event, since he seemed to understand.

Once the rodeo was over, the Snavely family left the bleachers for the last time and walked out past the closing concession booths.

Rodeo Surprise

Suddenly, Joy asked uncertainly, "Umm, Mommy, can we look at the horses before we leave? I know where they are; I saw them as we came in."

The horses were penned outside the arena. They were easily accessible, and Joy petted their soft noses. They were beautiful creatures; Joy observed their color and markings and labeled them as best she could, although Joy was no horse expert. All too soon, Joy had to pull herself away from gazing at the horses, so she and her family could go back to Grandaddy's house.

As she sat in the car, Joy hoped she would get to see more rodeos in the future. She hugged Geckie and told the little green lizard, "Well, Geckie, you're going to be my reminder of this special day, aren't you?"

Chapter 5

DIVING INTO SUMMER

"It's time to go home," announced Daddy on Thursday morning after breakfast.

"Thank you, Grandmama and Grandaddy," Joy and Ethan said. "We had a great time."

After everything was packed and all the goodbyes were said, the Snavelys left for home. On the trip, Joy and Ethan played with Spiny and Geckie. Skippy, the "monster" in Joy and Ethan's play world, was quite calm and certainly not anywhere near as ferocious toward the little geckos as they made him appear.

Soon, Mommy and Daddy began hearing things like "Hey, give me back Geckie!" or "Get your foot off me!" or "Ouch! Stop twisting my arm!" along with sounds of scuffling and tittering. This was what occasionally happened during long road trips. Though Joy and Ethan didn't really get hurt, Mommy said warningly, "Joy and Ethan, you need to stop."

They grew silent for a minute, but then started giggling again. Joy poked Ethan, he retaliated, and back and forth until Daddy spoke. "Hey! Your mommy told you two to stop," he said in a tone that produced immediate results; Joy and her brother became extremely quiet.

The rest of the trip was happily uneventful. The family arrived home in the afternoon. Joy raced upstairs and tossed her luggage on the floor. She set Geckie on her bed, where he joined Dolly; Harold the Elephant; Quiky-Quacky the Duck; and Fluffy the Teddy Bear.

The next morning, Joy went downstairs, plopped on the couch, and opened her well-worn Bible. Joy stroked Skippy while she read a chapter of Proverbs for that day. When she finished reading her Bible, Joy played with Skippy and tried to teach him to shake hands, but he never seemed to get the point of the lesson.

Joy walked into the kitchen and washed her hands in the sink. She took her cookbook out of the cupboard and began preparing sunny-side-up eggs, blueberry pancakes, and coffee. The coffee was particularly for Mommy.

Joy was in the middle of pouring pancake batter onto the griddle when she heard Mommy and Daddy coming into the kitchen. Joy turned and told her parents beamingly, "Good morning!"

"Mmm. Thank you for making breakfast for us. But...it looks like the eggs are burning," Mommy

46

remarked, reaching for a utensil. She was eyeing a crisp egg smoking under the pan lid. "Do you need any help?"

"*Please!*" Joy said gratefully.

Diving into Summer

Fifteen minutes later, Mommy and Joy had cleaned the kitchen and served breakfast. The food was good, except for the one egg that had been scorched. "Yuck!" Ethan exclaimed as he tasted the smoked egg, which unfortunately had been served to him. It was so strong it made his eyes water.

Daddy led the family devotion after Mommy and Joy washed the breakfast dishes. Devotion was on "Time with God." During devotion, Joy and Ethan took turns reading passages of Scripture, one of which was Jesus praying in the Garden. Joy felt pricked on hearing this devotional, because, although she read her Bible most mornings, she didn't pray as much as she should have. She realized it was important to pray to have the strength to do God's will in one's life.

Later in the day, Mommy ran some errands, so Daddy, Joy, and Ethan played video games. Joy did not get much accomplished: she kept messing up. After Joy's turn, Ethan played, but he didn't have much success either. In fact, he lost so many lives he got a "Game Over!"

Daddy, Joy, and Ethan took a break so they could have a snack. Joy made peanut butter and jelly sandwiches, and, in the process, left dirty plates and utensils in Mommy's clean kitchen sink. Joy wanted to keep playing with Daddy and Ethan upstairs, but she knew she shouldn't make more work for Mommy by leaving dishes for her to wash. At that moment, Joy remembered the Bible verse in James that told her if she knew the right thing to do, it would be sinning if she did not do it. With that, Joy easily repulsed the temptation to keep playing video games and went right into dishwashing. She even swept the kitchen floor after she was done!

After Joy finished her chore, she returned to play with Daddy and Ethan. As she went, she prayed, "Thank You, God, for giving me the strength to do the right thing by reminding me of Your Word."

When Mommy came home, Daddy, Joy, and Ethan stopped playing to help her bring in the groceries. When the groceries had been put away, Mommy prepared chicken-Alfredo pasta with creamy mashed potatoes. The meal was one of Joy's favorites! Joy helped Mommy stir the sauce, pour the penne into a saucepan, and turn the frying chicken.

The family played *Monopoly* that evening. All the property sets were quickly broken, however, so no one was the winner. It was a good thing the game finished early, though, because Joy had to go to bed at 7:30 p.m. since the next day, Saturday, held volleyball team tryouts at the YMCA.

At 6:30 a.m., Joy bounded out of bed ready for tryouts, although they weren't until 9:00 a.m. Joy quickly showered and put on a volleyball outfit Mommy had bought for her the day before.

Daddy drove the family to the YMCA, and dropped Mommy, Joy, and Ethan off near the door. Mommy checked in with Joy at the front desk.

Pushing open a big, heavy door, Joy entered the echoing indoor volleyball court. She stepped on a highly polished floor intersected by white and blue lines on her way to a group of girls her own age. They were listening to the coach, Mrs. Burgess, whom Joy found cheerful and encouraging. Joy set her water bottle and brand-new volleyball down on the floor and began running warm-up laps around the court at Mrs. Burgess's signal. The tryouts were drills of basic volleyball techniques, such as serving, bumping, setting, and spiking. Joy quickly learned how to hold out her arms to bump the ball into the air and how to set the ball for another team member to spike. At the end of tryouts, all the girls enjoyed a mini game of volleyball.

When tryouts were over, Mrs. Burgess told the girls, "Come back in two weeks for our first practice at 9:30 a.m. By then, you will all have been grouped into teams."

After leaving the YMCA, Daddy drove Joy to a sporting goods store to get knee pads, since she had been advised to get some for the first volleyball practice. After an unsuccessful search on their own, the family had to get store help to find the pads in a remote corner of the store.

On the way home, Mommy suddenly spoke up. "Joy?"

"Yes, Mommy?" Joy responded.

"I talked to Elizabeth's mother the other day, and she said Elizabeth could stay with us until the time to go to summer camp. Would you like me to invite Elizabeth?"

"Yes! Thank you!" Joy exclaimed.

Chapter 6

FRIENDS AND
INVITATIONS

Sunday, after church, Joy whizzed around the house, tidying up her room, pulling out games, and brushing Skippy. At 1:30 p.m., the doorbell rang. Joy, who had been choosing some movies to watch with her friend, jumped to her feet and raced to the front door. She opened the door, but all she saw was a package on the doorstep and a delivery truck driving away. "False alarm," Joy grumbled to Skippy, who barked and ran to the door whenever the doorbell rang. Disappointed, Joy took the package upstairs to Mommy, who was folding some clothes. She handed the box to Mommy and went back downstairs to finish organizing.

Finally, at a little past 2:00 p.m., the doorbell rang again. This time, Joy checked the small window near the door to make sure it was her friend. Sure enough, there was Elizabeth and her mother. Before Joy opened the door, she called Mommy to come downstairs.

"Hi, Joy!" said Elizabeth.

"Hey, Elizabeth! Thanks for coming over," Joy replied.

Elizabeth bent down to caress Skippy. She liked dogs—even barking ones. Unfortunately, Elizabeth couldn't have a dog of her own because her little sister was allergic to them.

While Mommy and Elizabeth's mother discussed a few things, the girls went upstairs to Joy's room. Elizabeth plopped her backpack on Joy's bed and laid her suitcase on the floor. The girls skipped back down the stairs to the living-room. Elizabeth said goodbye to her mother, then Mrs. Teller left.

Joy and Elizabeth popped popcorn and watched one of the movies that Joy had pulled out earlier. Ethan joined them to watch the movie *and* eat popcorn.

After watching the film, Elizabeth suggested they bake dessert. She and Joy asked Mommy, and Mommy said it was okay as long as they cleaned up afterwards. Joy took out her cookbook and flipped it to the dessert section.

Joy got a sudden inspiration as she leafed through the book. "Let's have a cookie-baking contest and see who can bake the best cookies *without* using a recipe!" she said.

Joy had a rough idea of how to make recipe-less cookies. The girls mixed crazy ingredients together and made a huge mess. When the cookies finally got into the oven, Elizabeth and Joy began to clean up. *Clang!* A large metal bowl crashed into the sink. Mommy came rushing down the steps, hoping that her dishes weren't broken. She heard giggling coming from the pantry. The door burst open, and Joy and Elizabeth tumbled out. When the timer for the cookies rang, Joy and Elizabeth carefully removed the cookies from the oven.

Daddy and Ethan were the appointed "taste testers." Elizabeth had made peanut butter cookies because she wanted Skippy to have some. Joy had added maple syrup and tons of dried fruit to her cookies. Daddy liked Joy's cookies better, although they were very sweet. Ethan, however, liked the peanut butter cookies. "Look!" Elizabeth said. "Skippy likes my cookies; he keeps begging for more!"

After their cookie contest, Joy and Elizabeth played *Uno* while eating more popcorn. After playing a few rounds, they played some card games that Elizabeth taught Joy.

"Can I play, too?" asked Ethan. The girls wanted to say "no," but, as they didn't want Ethan tattle-telling on them, they included Ethan in their games until it was almost his bedtime at 7:30 p.m.

Friends and Invitations

When it was almost *their* own bedtime, 8:00 p.m., Joy and Elizabeth packed up the cards and got ready for bed. Joy got out her devotional and read the Bible with her friend. They afterward climbed into Joy's big bed.

The next morning after breakfast, the girls went outside to play on the trampoline. They invited Ethan to play with them, and they all chased each other blindfolded and practiced tricks, like flipping and cartwheeling. Elizabeth knew the best tricks, and she and Joy taught Ethan a few of them.

While the children were taking a break, Joy suggested something else to do. "Hey, let's involve Skippy!"

"Can you bring me some water, too?" Ethan asked as Joy began zipping down the entrance of the trampoline.

Joy disappeared into the house and then reappeared carrying three bottles of water. Joy passed the bottles to Ethan, and she called Skippy. Skippy came at a canter, and Joy picked him up and set him in the trampoline. Ethan immediately started jumping, and Skippy slunk back to the exit. Skippy jumped down and trotted off. "Oh, great," muttered Joy, "Now I have to catch him again."

This time, however, Skippy knew that the children were going to put him back in the trampoline, so he hid underneath the trampoline. Joy dove in after him. She told Elizabeth and Ethan, "Please don't jump on top of me while I'm under here; *that's* gonna hurt."

Joy tried to catch Skippy, but he slipped out the other side. She chased Skippy around the yard and even cornered him once, but Skippy was too fast. Joy finally gave up, climbed into the trampoline, and resumed play.

"Time for lunch!" Mommy announced a half-hour later. Joy, Ethan, and Elizabeth bounded inside, washed their hands, and sat down at the table. Everyone prayed over their food and then took a bite of one of Mommy's deli sandwiches. Mommy also served a side of grapes, strawberries, and barbecue chips.

That Friday night, Joy and Elizabeth "camped out" in the living room. First, the girls pushed the couches together. Then they made a makeshift "tent" by stretching a large blanket over the couches and fastening it down with duct tape. The girls filled the space below with sheets, blankets, pillows, and stuffed animals. Unfortunately, there was always something coming loose, falling, or exposing yet another hole. To make matters worse, Skippy hopped in and brought down another part of the tent! Joy and Elizabeth quickly fixed up their tent with more tape, then settled down under their covers. They were so tired from the day's play that they soon drifted off to sleep.

Joy and Elizabeth woke up about six o'clock in the morning. They discovered that the makeshift tent had collapsed on top of them. "What a mess!" Joy exclaimed as she and Elizabeth crawled out of the tangle. They read a devotional together and then fed Skippy. Elizabeth gave Skippy a treat afterward.

Mommy soon came downstairs. "Make sure you clean up the living room," she told Joy.

"Yes, Mommy," Joy replied. However, thinking she would clean up later, she began helping Mommy with breakfast. Then, as the family was eating, Daddy stated that he wanted to have family devotion. After devotion, Daddy invited the girls and Ethan to play video games. They played until Daddy fell asleep, as he was quite tired from the week's work. The children sneaked out of the room and quietly shut the door. Then, the girls went to Joy's room and began preparing a tea party for their dolls.

"JOY!" Mommy's ominous voice suddenly sounded from downstairs.

"Oh, boy," thought Joy, gulping. "What did I do now?"

Joy yelled back, "Coming!" in a choked voice and rushed out of her room. She leaped down the steps at breakneck speed. Downstairs, Joy found Mommy glaring at her and pointing at the makeshift tent the girls had created. Joy meekly began picking up the bedclothes.

"For disobeying me," Mommy began, "You will pick this up—*yourself*—and put it in the washing machine. And once you finish that, you will fold all the clothes in the dryer."

Joy *immediately* did as she was told. She shoved the blankets into the washer, pulled out the clean clothes from the dryer, neatly folded them, and put them away.

When she finished, Joy apologized to Mommy. Mommy forgave Joy, but first gave her a little lecture on taking more responsibility with chores around the house. Finally, Joy was able to scurry back upstairs so she and Elizabeth could continue Dolly's tea party.

Chapter 7

CAMP PREPARATION

Wednesday night was church night. Mommy and Daddy went to the main service, Ethan went to Royal Rangers, and Elizabeth and Joy went to STARS class. STARS, a church organization that girls all over the United States could attend, taught lessons on subjects from cooking to salvation! Girls in STARS also filled in classwork sheets and memorized Bible verses.

The lead STARS teacher at Joy's church, Mrs. Falconer, made a major announcement that evening. "Girls, this is the final Wednesday before our camping trip on Friday. If you haven't done so already, please pick up a list of things you'll need for camp."

The camping trip to Conifer Lake Campground had been mentioned for several weeks already. Most of the girls in Joy's class, including Elizabeth, were planning to attend camp.

Mrs. Falconer gave out final camp instructions to the girls, reminding them, "You will need to be in the parking lot near our van around 11:30 a.m. on Friday."

Mrs. Falconer and Miss Sonner, an assistant STARS teacher, were going with eight girls from Joy's class to chaperone them. Different STARS classes from other churches in the surrounding district would be at camp as well.

The evening's lesson over the Fruit of the Holy Spirit was good, but Joy didn't hear much, as she was so excited about camp. Later that night, Joy even dreamed about the upcoming camping trip!

On Thursday, Mommy took Joy and Elizabeth last-minute shopping to buy needed items for the girls. Joy checked and re-checked her list to make sure that she had everything. Joy rolled her sleeping bag and mat together, packed a duffle bag to near bursting, and filled a backpack with little extras. Elizabeth took her sleeping bag and mat (rolled like Joy's) with her suitcase.

When Joy and Elizabeth woke up on Friday morning, a shiver of excitement ran through both of them. Mommy made waffles, and the girls helped her by washing the dishes in the sink.

When breakfast was over, Mommy and the girls got ready to leave. Meanwhile, Daddy gave Joy and Elizabeth some advice, and Ethan hinted that he wanted to go, too. However, it was a girls-only camp.

To pass the time during the drive to church, Joy looked through her things with Elizabeth. Her purse carried immediate necessities like tissue paper, chewing gum, a small mirror, and a few other things. Next, her backpack contained books, a notepad, and pencils. Joy's duffle bag held her clothes, toiletries, a lantern, and bigger things that would not fit elsewhere. Her sleeping bag had been rolled up with her blanket and pillow inside. Joy smiled in satisfaction, "Yep, that's everything—according to the list."

Joy hardly realized when they arrived at the church parking lot. Mommy found a parking space near the awaiting van. Joy hopped out and opened the trunk to take things out. Joy hugged Mommy and said, "Goodbye, Mommy; I love you." As Mommy kissed Joy, Joy felt a tinge of homesickness and tried to smile: she wasn't used to going places without her family.

Joy and Elizabeth found seats in the rear of the van. They sat together, buckled up their seat belts, and peered out the window. As the van roared to life and jerked out of the parking space, Joy waved one last time to Mommy. When the van turned onto the road, Joy could not see Mommy anymore.

Joy settled into her seat and set her purse and backpack beside her. Instead of reading books from her pack, as she usually would have done, Joy spent the hour-long ride talking with Elizabeth.

The ride was very bumpy. It seemed as if every imperfection in the road shook the van. The AC was extremely loud; Joy could hardly hear what Elizabeth said.

Finally, the van exited the interstate and traveled down a long, relatively empty highway. There were thick masses of trees on either side, making the area seem dark. A faded sign by the roadside claimed that Conifer Lake Campground was only half a mile away.

Before long, the van turned onto a dirt road leading to the camp and parked near the registration building. While Mrs. Falconer went inside to register, Miss Sonner allowed the girls to explore the area around the gravel parking lot.

Joy discovered the tiniest little toads. Most of them could easily sit on the eraser of a pencil! She excitedly called Elizabeth to see them. Elizabeth squealed with delight and pointed to one toad after another. Joy realized that the ground was swarming with them. She managed to catch one. Joy observed the toad for a moment, and then let him join his friends.

Finally, the girls in Joy's group were called together. They gathered their belongings and trekked to their cabin. As they walked along, the girls passed three cabins and a shower facility.

The group's cabin was made of pine boards and was set up on cinder blocks to keep it off the ground. Inside, there was a distinct piney smell. Two AC units hummed from different corners of the cabin. Rafters and hooks made perfect places to hang clothes and bags. Eight bunk beds were arranged in the cabin to make the most of the small space.

The girls dumped their heavy things on the floor and raced to claim the top bunks. Joy climbed up the ladder at the foot of her chosen bunk bed. Elizabeth found her spot next to Joy on the same bunk level.

Joy looked at her bed, which was covered with a teal-colored mattress. Like the cabin, it was simple yet sturdy. Mini rails on her bed could keep Joy from falling off in her sleep, but it couldn't stop her from stepping over to pay Elizabeth a visit!

From her perch, Joy observed the other girls looking for the most convenient beds. Miss Sonner was directly underneath Joy, and Mrs. Falconer had the bed under Elizabeth.

Miss Sonner suddenly called out, "Girls, you have one hour to set up your things! Then it's time for orientation." Joy left some of her things on her bed to claim her spot while she collected her remaining belongings from the van. Joy thought one hour was a long time, but she discovered she could not get everything organized before orientation.

Orientation was at a big fire pit outside the chapel building. As she walked down the short trail to the fire pit, Joy saw other girls from different churches. When all the groups arrived, everyone sat down on the benches around the fire pit.

Camp Preparation

A woman stood up and introduced herself as Miss Amelia. Miss Amelia welcomed all the girls and teachers. Then she gave a little speech about the reason for camp, which was learning about God's power in people. When she finished, some teachers helped Miss Amelia pass out booklets, name-tags, and camp T-shirts. After hanging her name-tag around her neck, Joy flipped through her booklet, which included several things: part of Miss Amelia's speech, the activity schedule, games such as tic-tac-toe, and pages for memoirs and notes.

Everyone's name-tag had a small sticker in one corner. Some stickers were red, others orange, yellow, green, or blue. All the girls were instructed to group together according to sticker color, and a leader for each color group would ask some icebreaker questions.

Joy, having an orange sticker, found herself in a group comprised mostly of people she didn't know. Only one or two girls from her church were there. Individually, the leader asked everyone in the orange group some questions such as "What is your favorite color?" "What is your favorite animal?" or "If you had a superpower, what would it be?"

After the icebreakers, Miss Amelia took everyone on a small tour of the Campground. Joy was especially curious to see the far side of the lake. The far side was more open, and Miss Amelia's house stood there.

The girls were dismissed to eat dinner at the Lakeview Dining Hall. The "Lake-to-be-viewed" was more like a large pond, but there was plenty of space in which to do some water activities.

Joy got in line at the buffet tables, served herself some food, and sat down next to Elizabeth. When everyone had filled their plates, Miss Amelia led in prayer over the meal. The girls said, "Amen," and began eating. Joy savored every bite of her food; it was so good it tasted homemade.

"It's almost time for chapel. You have five more minutes to finish," Mrs. Falconer said, seeing that most of her group had eaten. When the girls from Joy's group were ready, they walked to the chapel in the growing dusk and found seating.

The worship team began the service. A young woman sang hymns, and another played the guitar.

When they finished, Miss Amelia began reading 2 Timothy 1:6-7. She taught the girls about the Holy Spirit igniting adventure in them. She explained who the Holy Spirit was. To help illustrate, Miss Amelia took a special piece of paper and lit it with a match. She let the paper drop, and, while in midair, the piece of paper vanished! Some of the girls exclaimed in amazement. After her lesson, Miss Amelia concluded the service and dismissed the girls to make s'mores at the fire pit.

A crackling fire was going in the pit. Joy toasted some marshmallows for fun and watched them turn black and catch fire. Joy didn't care to eat marshmallows; however, she ate her share of chocolate and graham crackers.

When the girls left the fire pit, there was only one thing left to do before going to bed: visit the Snack Shack at the Lakeview Hall. Joy was glad she hadn't left her money at the cabin. She bought a bottle of juice and a small package of nuts.

Once the girls had made their purchases, Mrs. Falconer and Miss Sonner rounded up their group and took them to their cabin. Joy had her lantern with her, and helped light the way for her group, since the night had grown quite dark. A pile of gravel stood in their way. Joy stopped suddenly in front of the heap because, right on top of the gravel, sat a huge toad larger than Joy's hand! He was a giant compared to the little toads Joy had caught earlier. The other girls stood around, observing the big toad.

"I wish Ethan were here to see this," Joy remarked wistfully. The girls didn't have much time to admire the toad, though, because Mrs. Falconer whisked them off to the cabin.

Joy and her group went to the shower facility to brush their teeth and change into pajamas. The girls had to wait in line while other groups went in ahead of them. The shower facility was so small that Joy couldn't believe how thirty-five people on their side of the lake could ever get ready the next morning.

Once in her bunk, Joy went back to arranging her things. About 10:15 p.m., Miss Sonner got everyone's attention and told them, "It's time for devotion. Let's see how much you remember from Miss Amelia's presentation."

Joy answered discussion questions as well as she could and helped read Bible passages. After praying, Miss Sonner allowed the girls a little more time to play games or write in their journals.

While some of the girls played card games, Joy pulled out her notebook and camp booklet. Lights-out was at 11:00 p.m., so Joy had only about twenty minutes to journal. Joy wrote about the ride in the van and everything she had done so far at camp. She also drew sketches, though they were rather sloppy and "kindergarten-y."

Just before Joy wrote the last word in her journal, the lights went out. Some of the girls screamed a little. Then the lights came back on. Miss Sonner stood near the switch.

"I'll give you all a few minutes to get under your covers before I turn the lights off for good," Miss Sonner told the girls. Joy quickly wrote the last word, put away her journal, and dove under her blankets. She said goodnight to Elizabeth across from her and waited for the lights to "turn off for good." Even when they did, Joy still heard some chatter. "'Night, girls," Miss Sonner said firmly. The talk stopped as abruptly as if someone had turned off a radio.

Chapter 8

WEEKEND AT CAMP

The alarm on Miss Sonner's phone went off at 6:00 a.m. All the girls jolted awake. Joy sleepily groped for her bag and swung over the edge of the bunk bed. When they had gathered their things, the girls trekked up to the shower facility. Another long line greeted them. It didn't help that one of the three showerheads wasn't working properly. It took almost half an hour before Joy got to the head of the line, showered, and finished getting ready for the day. She wore her new camp T-shirt, as did many other girls.

While Joy waited for the teachers and remaining girls in her group to get ready, she explored more of the camp area with Elizabeth. They walked through a stand of fragrant conifers, fingering the pointy needles and admiring the scaly cones.

At 7:45 a.m., everyone was ready to head to the Lakeview Hall for breakfast. The buffet case displayed waffles, scrambled eggs, bacon, and orange juice. Joy helped herself to a good-sized portion of waffles and eggs.

After breakfast, there was chapel, during which time Miss Amelia continued her lecture on the Holy Spirit. The worship team stepped forward and led in the singing of more hymns. After chapel, the day's activities began.

The first thing on the schedule was a treasure hunt. The game worked this way: each group of girls received a differently-colored card with clues on it. Every group would follow the clues leading to the next card. The game continued until all nine cards of each color group were found. (The last card would lead to the chapel, where awards would be handed out to the first three groups to finish).

Joy raced with her friends to find the location of the next card. The eight girls found three cards together before they split up. The reason for splitting up was that they had found a card that was out of order. As a result, some girls went to find the cards in order, and others went to find different ones. Joy, Elizabeth, and another girl named Alice jogged on to find the next card. They found it behind a low wall.

They read the card and groaned when they saw that the directions led to the other side of the lake. Joy was tired of running. The three girls decided to join up with the others to see if they had found everything else.

"We have seven cards!" yelled Kimberly, a girl in Joy's group, "How about you?"

"We have one!" Joy cried. The remaining card happened to be the one on the other side of the lake.

To save time and energy, the girls planned a relay. Maria, yet another girl from Joy's group, would be stationed at the chapel door with the eight cards, while the others spaced out between the location of the last card and the chapel. Two girls hunted for the last card together. In five minutes, the two girls came sprinting back. They handed it to the first girl, Samantha, who in turn ran to the next girl. They continued until the last girl gave the card to Maria, who entered the chapel to turn in all the cards. Miss Amelia checked to make sure they had all nine. By this time, all the other girls in the group had arrived breathlessly.

"Good teamwork! You won second place," Miss Amelia announced.

"Congratulations, girls!" Miss Sonner, standing nearby, said proudly.

The girls received a little trophy for winning second place. Miss Sonner took a picture of the group with their trophy. She sent the picture to the girls' parents.

For the next activity, Miss Amelia divided all the girls into groups according to their age. The girls ages eleven to thirteen (including Joy) were in the Teal Group; the girls ages eight to ten went in the Pink Group; and the girls who were five to seven years of age were gathered into the Yellow Group.

The Teal Group went to Lakeview Hall to design vision boards. Vision boards were large pieces of white cardboard that the girls colored with markers and decorated with buttons cloth, and other craft items. They would decorate the boards according to a specific vision. For example, Joy chose foreign missions as her vision. She used colorful cloth to make a map of the world. Joy wrote in large letters across the top "Go Into All The World." She created all sorts of people holding hands out of more cloth and markers.

The teachers and girls around Joy kept saying, "Oh, I like your work!" or "That's very cool!" Joy didn't think her project looked as nice as others said, but she thanked them for their compliments.

Later on, Mrs. Falconer and Miss Sonner herded the vision-board-laden girls to their cabin to get ready for lunch. After the meal, the girls all prepared to go swimming in the lake.

Down by the lake, Joy took in her surroundings. The lake had been divided into sections for paddle boating, swimming, and canoeing. The area for paddle boats had a fountain in the middle that sprayed water in a smooth arc in many directions. The canoeing section had four or five canoes tied to the dock. A boathouse on the shore stored the canoe paddles and lifejackets. In the swimming section, a pier led down to the deeper water of the lake. A ladder went up to a tall diving board, and under it was "the blob." The blob was a huge float that one person sat on while someone else jumped on it from the diving board, launching the other person into the air. The swimming section also had a water trampoline and jungle gym.

After fitting on their lifejackets, Joy consented to ride in a paddleboat with Elizabeth. Both pumped their legs to get the boat going toward the middle of the lake.

While they were under the fountain, Joy piped up with an idea. "Hey! Let's paddle as fast we can back to the dock. I'll get another paddleboat, and we'll have a race."

"Okay—ready, set, GO!" Elizabeth yelled. The two girls pumped faster and harder. The boat's paddle churned and splashed in the water. Joy felt her energy drain in a flash. She and Elizabeth gave themselves a break before long.

"Whew, that was hard!" Joy exclaimed when they got back to the dock.

"Yeah, let's drop the race idea; I wanna go swim," Elizabeth replied.

Joy and Elizabeth refreshed themselves in the cool, green water, then swam to the big water trampoline. A slide on one side of it allowed people to get off the trampoline without jumping into the water.

Joy went a full circle around the water trampoline before finding the tiny ladder that went four feet up to the top. Joy and Elizabeth tried to go up the ladder at the same time, but it was very flimsy. Joy lost her balance, swung off the ladder, and landed back in the water. "Whoa!" she shouted.

By the time Joy came back to the surface, Elizabeth was already bouncing on the trampoline. Joy successfully climbed the ladder the second time.

Some other girls tried to climb up the water trampoline as well, but most met with similar fates as Joy. Joy and Elizabeth offered to help. Once, Elizabeth was pulled off when a girl misstepped and fell over backward!

When Joy and Elizabeth tired of playing on the trampoline, they slipped down the slide and made their way to the water jungle gym. It was rather hard work to climb up the contraption. Joy and Elizabeth eventually made it to the top, where they sat down to take in the view.

"Let's go back down," Joy said, "We can try out the 'blob.'"

Elizabeth and Joy descended the jungle gym carefully until they reached a spot where they could safely jump off. They held each other's hand and plunged into the water.

Joy sank like a stone into the cold and murky depths. She quickly came back into the warmer water, however, and rose above the surface with a gasp for air. Joy shivered and looked at the goose bumps on her arms. "Brr-r. T-t-that water gets really c-c-cold," Joy said as her teeth chattered, "I'm g-g-going to get m-my towel."

With that, Joy swam to the pier and climbed up the metal ladder to the deck. The sunbaked pier felt burning hot to Joy's feet. She winced to her flip-flops, put them on, and wrapped herself in her large towel, which was deliciously warm from the heat of the sun. Joy lay down on one of the lawn chairs nearby and planned to stay only until she felt the chilliness from the water go away. She closed her eyes and listened to the sounds of activities around her.

A few moments later, Joy heard something rustling. She opened her eyes to see Elizabeth sitting on the chair beside her.

"So, uh, when are we going back?" Elizabeth queried. "Oh, in a minute or two," Joy replied, closing her eyes again.

Moments later, Elizabeth grew restless. "See ya, Joy! I'm going onto the blob," she exclaimed.

Joy watched as Elizabeth was thrown eight feet into the air by the blob. Joy felt she was missing out on some fun, so she ran to the end of the blobbing line.

When Joy's turn came, she scurried up the tall ladder to the diving board. She jumped, hit the "blob," and watched the girl she had "blobbed" fly up and land in water. Brianna, a girl from Joy's group, asked Joy, "Can I blob you?"

Joy nodded, then swam over to the end of the blob to sit on it. It was harder to get up on than she expected. When Joy had finally caught hold, she shut her eyes as Brianna came down.

Joy blobbed and got blobbed several times before deciding to move on to the next activity—canoeing. She looked for Elizabeth but couldn't find her.

Weekend at Camp

Oh well, I'll go canoeing with someone else, she thought. Joy found an empty canoe near the shed and invited Maria and a girl from a different church to go with her. A camp attendant gave them some paddles and untied the canoe from the dock. The girls all piled in and pushed off.

The funny thing about the canoeing venture was that Joy and her small group kept bumping into the exact same canoe at least five times. "Oh, no! Not again!" groaned the girls in the other canoe before the sixth collision. This time, Joy finally managed to change course at the last second.

A piercing whistle broke the sounds of chattering, shrieking, and laughing. "Time to bring it in, girls!" shouted Miss Amelia. Joy and her companions began paddling their canoe over to the dock. Maria however, began arguing with the other girl over which way to go, and the canoe drifted through the buoys that marked the barrier between the canoeing and swimming sections. Joy, noting the situation, paddled furiously to get out of the swimming section before anyone noticed. Joy maneuvered the canoe to the dock, where a camp attendant helped her tie the canoe and step out onto shore.

Joy put on some clothes over her swimsuit, but she was still rather damp and chilly as she sat in Lakeview Hall doing Badges. Badges were simply a camp continuation of STARS class. Joy diligently completed her classwork and quoted a memorized Bible verse to her teacher.

After Badges, the groups were given two hours to shower and rest in the cabins. Afterwards, they could go behind Lakeview Hall to play some games.

First, there was tetherball. One girl hit the ball to get it to wind around the pole. Then another girl tried to counterattack and get the ball to go the other way. The girls played until the ball came off the cord!

Then the girls switched to playing dodgeball inside a circular fence—like a small corral. The way the game worked was this: one girl was chosen to stand in the center holding a playground ball. The other girls would stand in a circle within the fence perimeter. The girl holding the ball would throw it at the others. They would scatter, trying to avoid the ball. If someone got hit, she was "out" and had to leave. Play would continue until only one person was left. The winner would begin the next round with the ball.

After playing games, the girls went to supper. Joy filled her plate with a big square of steaming-hot lasagna and a couple of tongs-full of Caesar salad. Dessert was chocolate-covered ice cream bars.

Chapel was right after supper. Joy was moved by the service and went to the altar crying. She spent some time praying that God would use her for His will.

Once chapel ended, there was not much left of the day. It was 8:20 p.m. The Snack Shack was open again, and Joy bought a package of chewing gum.

Back at the cabin, there was devotion and a few minutes to play. Joy wrote in her journal about the day's events. By 10:30 p.m., it was lights-out. Snug in her bed, Joy thanked God for everything she had done that day. Tired, she drifted off to sleep.

The alarm rang at 7:30 the next morning. Because they needed to be at breakfast by 8:00 a.m., Mrs. Falconer decided that they would have to skip showering that morning. Joy didn't like the idea of not being able to shower all day, but there was no choice.

Cereal cups, fruit, and toast made up the breakfast menu that morning. For dessert, there were strawberries for dipping in a chocolate fountain.

Chapel started immediately after breakfast. Joy and Elizabeth were moved to tears by the Holy Spirit, and Miss Sonner prayed with them. Chapel lasted an hour, during which time Joy remained in God's presence.

Afterwards, the girls were dismissed to go to the sand pit to play messy games, which turned out not so messy after all! The girls in the Teal Group split into two teams. Each group formed a ring by holding hands. A hula-hoop was put between two girls in each team. When the teacher said "Go," the first girl would step through the hoop and pull her head through, or vice versa. The first team to get the hoop all the way around the ring of girls won. The catch was that if the ring broke by someone letting go, the team would have to restart. Joy's team won four times, while the other team enjoyed seven victories.

Next, the Teal Group moved on to crafts. Seated at some of the tables in the back room of the Lakeview Hall, the girls got ready to make bracelets.

Joy received a sheet of instructions and a kit bag. Joy opened the bag and began twisting together the little rings and beads. When she adjusted her bracelet to the length she wanted, Joy put on the final clasp. Her bracelet was almost finished; she just needed to add little trinkets to it. Joy chose two different pieces that had the words LOVE and ADVENTURE on them. Lastly, Joy found a trinket that had her birthstone color on it—a ruby. Joy fastened on her bracelet with Elizabeth's help and found it to be a worthy keepsake.

After crafts, the Teal Group went to another Badges class. Joy completed her requirements early and waited for the rest of the girls to finish. To pass the time, Joy helped the teachers put away supplies.

Lunch was served soon after; it was to be the last meal of camp. The buffet table displayed fried chicken, vegetables, and tomato soup. Joy slowly ate the last bites of food.

The last chapel service occurred right after lunch. The girls sang worship songs and listened to Miss Amelia's final lecture on the Holy Spirit.

The day soon ended after chapel. By this time, the girls were beginning to feel tired and homesick. Most of them, including Joy, started getting a little crabby. It was definitely time to leave for home.

Back at the cabin, Joy began packing the things on her bunk bed. Joy found that things didn't fit quite as neatly as when she had first packed them, but Joy wasn't about to redo everything. She hung her bags over her shoulders and carried her vision board and sleeping bag in front of her.

Finally, the room was cleared. The girls lined up at the door and tramped outside. Miss Sonner led in front and Mrs. Falconer followed behind. Mrs. Falconer scanned the room, turned off the lights, and shut the door.

Miss Sonner unlocked the van and started it. The girls piled their bags in the back of the van and flopped into their seats, waiting for Mrs. Falconer to check out of the camp.

Joy recorded the day's events in her journal while the van rumbled on its way to the interstate. Joy discovered that Elizabeth, seated next to her, had fallen asleep on her shoulder. Before she knew it, Joy was asleep as well.

About forty-five minutes later, Joy felt the van roll to a stop. She opened her eyes to see they had just exited the interstate and were waiting for the traffic light to change. "Hey, wake up, Elizabeth," Joy whispered as she gently poked her friend.

"Where are we?" Elizabeth asked, yawning.

"I think it's Exit 86," Joy replied.

"Oh, good, that means we're close."

The van chugged on for a couple of minutes longer, then the big, white church burst into view. Joy looked at the handful of cars in the parking lot, searching for Mommy's car. When the van was parked, Joy and all the girls scrambled out. Mommy and Ethan came out of the car to meet Joy, and Joy hugged them tightly.

"I'm so glad to be back!" Joy exclaimed.

Mommy opened the trunk of the SUV, and Ethan helped the girls with their bags. When Joy got inside the car, she noticed a flower bouquet with a card. Joy picked up the flowers and sniffed their sweet fragrance. She opened her card and read Mommy's sweet message.

"Oh, thank you, Mommy. It's so beautiful!"

Joy was bursting to recount her camp adventure to Mommy, but she saved it until the whole family could hear so she wouldn't have to repeat the story.

Once at home, Daddy and Skippy greeted Joy. Joy gave Daddy a big hug and then tried to calm Skippy. He was wild with excitement to have Joy back. Joy and Elizabeth went upstairs and dumped their bags on the floor of Joy's room. Then the girls took turns taking a long, hot shower.

After that, the family gathered around the dinner table to share a bowl of tortilla chips and salsa, listen to Elizabeth and Joy's story, and have devotion. When the family was done, it was nearly 8:00 p.m.—bedtime.

Chapter 9

BOATING AND "BOLLEY-BALL"

Elizabeth stayed with Joy and her family until Tuesday, when Elizabeth's parents picked her up. Joy soon started volleyball practice. Her team named themselves the Fireballs and chose a bright orange for their jersey color. Joy liked warm-up time when she and her team would jog two laps around the court. Joy tried to pass as many people as she could without cutting corners. Joy played rather well, yet her weak points were serving overhand and spiking. The team focused on repetitive drills and mini-games.

Joy met her cousin Cassie at volleyball. Cassie had been out of state all summer visiting relatives. Cassie's parents were Uncle Doug (Daddy's brother) and Aunt Kim. When Cassie had gotten back from the visit, she signed up for volleyball with Joy.

After Joy's third volleyball practice, Daddy took advantage of a three-day weekend for D-Day to take his family on a boating trip. Early that Friday morning, Joy woke up to hear the front door slam: it was Daddy. Joy sneaked out of her room and peered down the stairwell. Daddy was already gone.

Joy then went to the master bedroom and knocked on the door. "Mmmm, yes?" answered Mommy groggily. Joy cracked the door open and slipped through. "Mommy, where did Daddy go?" Mommy didn't answer; she only motioned Joy to get in bed. Joy crawled in next to Mommy and soon fell asleep.

The warm yellow sunlight peeked into the room and woke Joy. Joy lay in bed for a minute, but then she heard Mommy's voice floating up from downstairs. Daddy was also with her. Joy leaped out of bed and went to her own room.

The family was ready and in the car by 7:30 a.m. Joy and Ethan had been told they were going boating on Stillhouse Hollow Lake. Beach towels, a lunch cooler, and sunscreen were piled in the seat between Joy and Ethan.

When they reached the Marina, the family parked, got out, and walked to a blue truck a couple of parking spaces away. A man in the driver side of the truck got out and began talking with Daddy. He had rented Daddy a pontoon boat earlier in the morning. The man introduced himself as Mr. Roscoe.

Mr. Roscoe led the family over to the *Belle*, a boat that the family was to take on their excursion. After some instructions on operating the boat, Mr. Roscoe left.

Daddy took the keys and started the boat. He began edging out of the dock and out of the little inlet. Meanwhile, Joy helped Mommy put things away in the handy compartments under the seats. In the back, Joy found some fishing rods and an inner tube; she was excited about riding that inner tube. The brilliant morning sun threw sparkles on the deep blue water. Little whitecaps were whipped up by the fresh breeze, and gulls glided overhead.

Out on the open water, Daddy went as fast as he could go and swung the boat to the right and left. "Whee!" "Woo-hoo!" Joy and Ethan gave out whoops of delight as Daddy spun the boat around. One time, Joy thought she would get thrown out of the boat.

In a quiet, shaded cove, Daddy stopped the boat and had Ethan drop anchor. It was a good spot for fishing. The family baited some lines and cast them into the water. They all waited a long time to get a bite. They even checked their hooks every so often, but only Joy's line had a missing piece of bait.

After an hour, the family realized that the fishing venture had been a failure. They reeled in their lines and set them aside. Even before going fishing, Joy had a feeling that no one was going to catch anything.

Gliding out of the cove and along the shoreline, Daddy found a rocky beach on a small island. He steered the boat and let it run ashore. Everyone thought it was a good idea to do some exploring on the island.

Joy jumped out of the boat and tried to land clear of the water. She sat on a large rock with Mommy and watched Daddy and her brother pull the boat in closer to shore. They planted the anchor as deeply as it would go.

Before leaving the boat, Mommy made certain to put sunscreen on the children. Joy and Ethan reluctantly stayed put while Mommy rubbed the lotion on their arms, legs, and faces. Joy and Ethan didn't particularly care for the smell of the sunscreen and squirmed when Mommy accidentally got it in their eyes.

Daddy led the way up the island. There were no trails. Briars, cacti, and the branches of scrub trees barred the family's way. To top it all off, the day had turned very hot.

The trek took the family to the summit of the island, which turned out to be a peninsula. From that point, the boat could not be seen, since it was hidden from view by a clump of trees. Without much to do at the top of the peninsula, the family decided to turn around and head to the beach.

Boating and Bolley-Ball

The family came out of the brush to find that the boat was drifting away! It was out of swimming range, and the only option was to walk along the winding beach and hope to meet the boat as it floated past, pushed by the wind.

The briars had scratched Joy's arms and legs, and her shoes were covered with prickly burrs inside and out. She was miserably dirty, thirsty, and ready to cry. The family tramped down the beach, and soon Daddy and Ethan pulled ahead quite a distance.

Mommy put her comforting arms around Joy, who had tears streaming down her face. "What's wrong, Joy?" Mommy asked. The welling emotions inside Joy finally burst forth. "We—won't—find—the boat—a-and—all our things…"

Joy hiccupped between choked gasps for air. Joy couldn't finish what she was about to say because just then she went into a fresh round of sobbing. Mommy told her that they needed to have faith that God had already helped them find the boat. *("God, I pray that we will get to the boat in time. I will put our family devotion into practice by having faith and thanking You that You've already helped us.")*

Joy was barely getting over her meltdown when she came across something that almost made her jump out of her skin! Less than two feet from her, Joy saw the skeleton of a rotting fish. Not only did Joy find skeletons creepy, she also nearly stepped on this one. Joy shot up into the air with a horrified scream, "Eek!" She came down stamping her feet. After passing the thing, Joy did not venture to look back.

When Mommy realized what had happened, she started laughing so hard she broke into a fit of coughing. "It's not funny," Joy muttered, feeling her face get warm. She scowled and stared at her shoes while she walked. In a minute, Joy also realized that it actually was quite hilarious. Suddenly, both Mommy and Joy were giggling about the incident.

Quite contrary to Joy's previous forebodings, Daddy and Ethan did manage to catch the runaway *Belle*. By the time Mommy and Joy arrived, Daddy and Ethan were chugging bottles of water on deck.

Once everyone had settled down, the family resumed the water activities. It was time to get on the inner tube! Joy let Ethan go first. She watched as Ethan threw out the tube, descended the small ladder at the back of the boat, and climbed onto the inner tube. The long rope slowly grew taut as Daddy edged the boat forward. Daddy was soon going full speed. The family laughed as Ethan's legs jounced every which way.

About five minutes later, Daddy stopped and allowed Ethan to reel himself in. Once on the boat, Ethan helped Joy get down onto the inner tube. Joy held tightly to the handles and waited for Daddy to gain speed. She turned her head to the side so she wouldn't smash her nose. The little float she rode bounced with every wave, especially on the boat's wake.

Joy and Ethan made several exchanges so both got plenty of turns on the inner tube. After a while, Joy decided to sit down instead of lie down on the tube. This time, when Daddy started, Joy went underwater. Joy watched as the water slowly rose and covered her completely. The water went up her nose before she had time to react. Then, as quickly as she had gone down, Joy came back to the surface coughing and spluttering. Joy's throat stung, and the inside of her nose smarted. Joy had stayed underwater for only a second, but it felt much longer than that. When Daddy noticed what was happening, he stopped to let Joy catch her breath. After that, whenever Joy rode on the inner tube, she lay down flat.

After the family turned in the boat late that afternoon, Joy thanked Daddy for the day's adventure. As they drove home, each family member shared their favorite part of the day and thanked God they had found the boat.

Joy's first volleyball game was scheduled for Saturday evening. The day finally came, and dusk started to fall as the family arrived at the YMCA. As customary, Daddy dropped off Mommy, Ethan, and Joy near the entrance.

Inside the court, Joy got a ball from the basket and began practicing serves. Joy could only serve underhand well, but she tried some overhands to see if she could get the ball over. Surprisingly, one overhand serve did make it!

During warm-up and volleyball practice, the small bleachers around the court began filling up with relatives and friends of the volleyball players. After ten minutes of practice were up, a referee blew his whistle. Everyone on Joy's team gathered around Mrs. Burgess, who assigned positions and gave the girls a pep talk. She also chose a team captain. The Fireballs were given first serve. The team put their hands together and chanted, "One, two, three, Fireballs!"

The game began, and the Fireballs' best server executed a beautiful overhand. The volleyball sailed to the other side, where the other team, the Hurricanes, bumped and set the ball back over the net. One of the Fireballs tried to set as well but failed to hit the ball hard enough.

Joy got in a couple of good hits on the ball (including some "backward" hits) and served twice in a row. She could hear Daddy yelling from the bleachers as she served an ace. Joy, now a little overconfident, made her third serve an overhand, but it fell far short of the net.

During the first half of the game, Joy's team was ahead: 13 to 11. However, the Fireballs lost the game: 24-19. "It's okay," Mrs. Burgess said reassuringly. "There are plenty of games left in the season. You all did so well. Let's go and give the other team high fives."

The Fireballs and Hurricanes lined up on opposite sides of the net and walked towards each other. Every team member gave a rapid high five and a mumbled "good game."

After collecting her things, Joy joined her family. Daddy gave her a strong high five and a "Yeah!"

"Can I have some ice cream?" Joy asked.

"Me, too!" Ethan chimed in.

Daddy obligingly took the family out for ice cream at the nearest ice cream shop. Standing in front of the glass case, Joy could hardly decide what flavor she wanted. She settled on peanut butter and banana ice cream mixed together, along with a sprinkle of mini chocolate chips. Joy savored the blended flavors and crunched on the chocolate chips in her mix.

At home, Joy was just about to get in bed before she remembered something. She bounded out of her room, ran to her parents' door, and knocked. Daddy came out from around the corner and asked, "Yes?"

"Daddy," Joy began, "I forgot to thank you for the ice cream and for taking me to the game. So, er…thank you."

"You're welcome. But get to bed; it's way past your bedtime."

"Yes, sir. Goodnight, Daddy. I love you."

Joy lay in her bed waiting for Mommy to come. Mommy never missed saying goodnight to Joy or Ethan for as long as Joy could remember. Joy was just about to drift off to sleep when her door creaked open. Mommy came, kissed Joy, and whispered, "Remember to pray." Joy nodded in response and breathed, "I love you." After Mommy left, Joy thanked God for the day and then went to sleep.

Chapter 10

MID-SUMMER

On Monday afternoon, Joy and Ethan helped Mommy clean up the messy garage. Little by little, as things were stacked in wrong places, the garage had become what Mommy called a "tornado aftermath." Along with cleaning up and organizing, Mommy wanted to donate things the family no longer used.

Joy was looking through some old boxes when she saw something wedged between two tall boxes. As she wrenched it out, Joy saw it was their camping tent they had misplaced during the last move! Joy called Ethan and showed him her discovery. They both instantly got an idea.

"Mommy?" Joy ventured. "Can we sleep in the backyard inside the tent? With Skippy, too?" Mommy smiled and told them they could.

Later in the day, with the garage cleaned, dinner eaten, and the tent set up, Joy and Ethan made their final preparations. They brought flashlights, sleeping bags, pillows, blankets, games, and Skippy. They threw their things inside and began arranging them, while Skippy sat on a pile of bedding watching Joy and Ethan the whole time.

Joy and Ethan played some games, but it quickly became too dark to see. Then Joy and Ethan set their games aside and tussled with Skippy a bit.

At the last minute, despite Ethan's objections, Joy decided to take the tarp off the top of the tent so she could see the stars. However, it was the *stars* that were soon seeing a sleeping girl, a sleeping boy, and a sleeping dog.

Before dawn, Joy began dreaming. She dreamt that she was standing in a field full of dandelions. The whole field was soaked with dew. Ethan was standing in front of Joy, and he began throwing wet flowers at her. Joy could do nothing whatsoever to stop Ethan. He just kept tossing them at her and making her feel damp and chilly.

Suddenly waking from her dream, Joy sat up in her sleeping bag just to get sprayed in the face with water! It was the lawn sprinkler system that had turned on according to schedule!

"Ugh," Joy said as the water came back around. No wonder she dreamed she was getting wet! Joy dove under the soggy blankets to reach the only dry spot on the floor of the tent. By now, Ethan was awake and hiding under his covers. Skippy had also gotten to his feet and was trying to shake the water out of his fur.

"I knew you shouldn't have taken the cover off the tent," Ethan griped. "If you hadn't, we wouldn't be wet."

After fifteen minutes, the sprinkler system finally turned off. Joy and Ethan decided that the best course of action was to collect everything and go inside the house.

Joy and Ethan heaped their things on the living room floor and stretched out to sleep on the couches. Joy invited Skippy to join her on the sofa; he jumped onto the couch and curled up next to Joy.

Joy woke up again around 6:30 a.m. Skippy was partly on her, with the top of his head under Joy's chin. Joy remained still so as not to bother Skippy. Her memory captured the moment, and, for a long time afterward, Joy remembered those special moments with her dog.

In a while, however, Joy became uncomfortable. She stirred, and just as she had suspected, Skippy got up. Joy found no reason to stay asleep any longer, so she rolled out of her makeshift bed. She threw the dirty blankets into the washer and woke up Ethan. Joy stuffed his things into the washer as well.

Joy and Ethan then each read their Bibles. Joy managed to memorize Philippians 4:8, The verse with the good things on which Christians should think. Joy wanted to memorize the verse because it had been in yesterday's devotion. Joy had previously known Philippians 4:8 by heart, but when Daddy had asked her during devotion to quote it, she didn't even remember the first word. As a result, Daddy and Ethan teased her for forgetting the verse, and Joy had been so embarrassed she purposed to learn it again the next day.

After saying it correctly to herself, Joy asked Ethan to listen to her recite the verse. Ethan told her that she got it right, and, when Daddy came home from work that day, Joy proudly told Philippians 4:8 to him.

Mommy didn't feel well the following morning. She had a bad headache that made her stay in bed. When Joy and Ethan got up, the kitchen lights weren't on usual. Joy and Ethan went to Mommy's room to investigate, but they soon left to let her rest when they saw she was not well.

After standing aimlessly around the kitchen island, Joy got an idea. She shared it with Ethan, and he agreed. Why didn't they help Mommy today without her knowing it? Joy emptied the dishwasher and prepared a small breakfast, while Ethan took out the trash and swept the front entrance. Joy and Ethan tried to do their tasks quietly so they didn't wake Mommy again.

Joy and Ethan ate their breakfast of scrambled eggs and buttered toast while coffee bubbled in the percolator. When the coffee was ready, they poured it and set it next to Mommy's breakfast. Joy and Ethan also left handwritten notes next to Mommy's plate.

It took another forty-five minutes for Mommy to wake up, so Joy and Ethan played a board game while they waited. When Mommy finally came out of her room, the breakfast, which had once been steaming hot, was quite cold. Nevertheless, Mommy was so happy with Joy and Ethan's thoughtfulness she almost cried. As Mommy reheated the breakfast, she thanked Joy and Ethan for letting her rest, because now she was much better.

Joy and Ethan were glad they had helped Mommy, and, later that day, Mommy made them *flan*. *Flan* was a custard-like dessert made of evaporated and condensed milk, cream cheese, and eggs that had been blended together and baked in a water bath. While Joy ate her piece of *flan*, she remembered how she had read in her Bible that if one gave, it would be returned in overflowing measure. Joy applied the truth today. She had given Mommy breakfast, and Mommy gave her a sweet treat in return.

Joy spent her week playing volleyball and enjoying her free time, but she looked forward to doing something special with Daddy for Father's Day.

Joy woke up early on Father's Day. She found Daddy downstairs taking his vitamins.

"Vitamins first!" Daddy said when he saw Joy going past the vitamin closet.

Joy immediately went to him and held her mouth open while he popped two vitamin gummies into it.

"Happy Father's Day, Daddy!" Joy told him when she had cleared enough space in her mouth.

About ten minutes later, Ethan and Mommy had awakened as well. Ethan also had his vitamins. Daddy then asked Joy and Ethan if they wanted to go on an adventure with him. The children eagerly said they did. Mommy began cooking a nutritious breakfast of oatmeal, scrambled eggs, and cheese toast.

About half an hour after leaving the house, Daddy entered Fort Hood. First, he stopped at the nearest gas station and filled up the vehicle's tank. He took Joy and Ethan inside the store to get something to drink. Daddy bought two bottles of sports drinks for himself. Daddy drained his two containers before Joy could drink one-fourth of her bottle!

Daddy drove the children to Brigadier Field, where an Army challenge course was. Various obstacles were scattered across the green, manicured lawn.

The first challenge was Log Steps. It consisted of about a dozen logs lined up in a row. They were set up waist high. To complete the course, a person had to throw his leg over the first log, sort of straddle the log, and then bring his other leg to the other side. It was similar to slow-motion hurdles in a race.

Joy and Ethan took the challenge, and Joy won by a hair. There were more challenges in Brigadier Field, as well as other courses in different fields around the military base.

Joy's favorite course of the day was a rope climb. It looked like the skeleton of a small A-frame house with ropes intersecting each other where the sidewalls should have been. When Daddy said "Go," Joy leapt up and used her hands and feet as if she were climbing a ladder. When she got to the top, Joy scurried back down the other side. She clearly beat Ethan in that challenge. Joy liked the climb so much, she asked to do it again.

When the children finished monkeying around on the courses, Daddy took Joy and Ethan to the clothing store to get a "souvenir." Joy chose a magenta T-shirt that had the word ARMY on it in large, white lettering.

As Joy wandered around the store, she caught sight of some plush animals. Joy spun the rack around nonchalantly until she saw little gray elephants. She caught one up and looked at it. It had on a tiny, bright pink shirt. Joy cuddled the plush toy, then went to find Daddy. Daddy was near the checkout line choosing between different kinds of laser lights with Ethan.

"Daddy," Joy began, holding up the elephant, "Can I have this?"

Daddy looked and said, "All right." Joy took his answer as a yes. She and Ethan put their things on the conveyor belt. Meanwhile, Joy thought of good names for her new plush toy. In the car, Joy came up with an idea.

"Do you think Daisy would be a good name for her?" Joy asked Ethan. "Sure. Why not? Sounds good to me," Ethan replied.

"Daisy," Joy murmured to the stuffed animal. She made the little elephant's head nod, gesturing acceptance to the name.

Mid-Summer

Chapter 11

OCEAN PARK ADVENTURE

The next Saturday, Mommy told Joy and Ethan to pack their swimsuits, hats, sunscreen, and towels in a bag. Joy crammed her backpack with the things Mommy told her to bring. Everyone was out the door twenty minutes later.

Daddy locked the front door behind him and opened the trunk of Mommy's car. It was still quite early when Joy looked at the clock on the car's dashboard: the time was 8:30 a.m.

Joy pressed her face to the window of the car to look up at the high-flying clouds scuttling by in the clear, blue sky. The fields around were dotted with cattle grazing and resting. Joy suddenly caught sight of something out of the corner of her eye. She tugged Ethan's shirt and motioned him to see a racer-type car next to them on the highway. It was a bright orange color and had a spoiler. "Wow!" Ethan exclaimed.

Talking passed the time, but Joy and Ethan ran out of things to say to each other. They then asked Mommy if they could play on her phone, and Mommy said they could on the condition they only play thirty minutes each. Joy quickly set a timer for thirty minutes, then she and Ethan were soon bending over Mommy's phone, lost in their game. When Joy's timer rang, Joy passed the phone to Ethan. Ethan played for another half hour.

When they stopped gaming, Joy and Ethan realized they were traveling through a city—San Antonio, in fact. They also began seeing signs for Ocean Park, a large waterpark. Excitement grew in Joy and Ethan.

Less than ten minutes later, Daddy was already in the parking lot. The family found a space to park, got out their bags, and went to the entrance that read "OCEAN PARK" in huge letters. Joy and Ethan's initial excitement was dampened when they saw the long lines of people waiting to get inside the park. There was to be one hour of standing…and standing. Joy and her family finally reached a ticket booth, where (after Daddy paid for four people) Joy and Ethan received park maps. Unfortunately, Joy soon lost her map to a puddle of dirty water and had to share a map with Ethan until she could get another one later.

The family came to a shallow pool full of stingrays. At a ray-feeding stand, Daddy bought Joy and Ethan some small frozen fish to feed the stingrays. Ethan soon mastered the trick of feeding the stingrays efficiently. Joy looked over at Ethan and watched him successfully give stingrays food. Joy was struggling to give the stingrays her fish. Ethan laughed when he saw Joy putting her fish directly in *front* of the stingrays. No wonder she was having a hard time! Ethan came over and showed Joy how to do it correctly. He reminded his sister that a stingray's mouth is *beneath* it. Since Joy felt uneasy putting her hand under a stingray, she gave Ethan the rest of her fish.

Once the fish ran out, Joy and Ethan threw away their containers and went on with Mommy and Daddy to the Whale Arena. They found good seats on the bleachers; even though the show would begin in minutes, not a whole lot of people were around.

There was an enormous tank of water opposite Joy and her family which sloshed up water every so often. Joy was almost staggered at the thought of the possible dimensions and capacity of the whale arena. Above the water, there was a large screen which gave a slideshow of whale and dolphin facts. A circular platform at the level of the water was under the big screen. On either side of the platform were water gates which would allow aquatic animals to pass through when opened.

As Joy looked at her surroundings, she noticed some signs marking the extent of a "splash zone." (Joy and her family were just above this zone.) Joy wondered how and why water would be able to reach so far, but she would soon find out!

Soon, Joy began seeing whales surfacing on the other side of the gate, impatient to get out into the arena. In a few minutes, the gates opened, and a group of dolphins, porpoises, and beluga whales came surging out. Trainers stepped out onto the platform, greeting the audience, and began giving the whales cues for tricks, such as jumping, waving, "talking," and coming onto the platform. These marine animals performed tricks in synchrony with music coming over loudspeakers.

One cool trick the belugas did was to sweep across the perimeter of the tank, using their flukes to create massive waves behind them. Cold water spilled over onto the crowd below amid exclamations of surprise.

It was then that Joy began to realize what the "splash zone" was about, but that wasn't all. By and by, the porpoises and beluga whales left, and the dolphins remained. They were sent to the edge of the tank, where they began to slap the water with their powerful tails and send more sprays at the spectators.

Joy and her family must have chosen their seats well because hardly a drop of water reached them. On the other hand, people within the "splash zone" were entirely soaked.

Ocean Park Adventure

The finale of the dolphin show was spectacular. The dolphins jumped extra high now, with amazing corkscrew turns and flips. They patterned their jumps in duos and trios, until the end, where all seven dolphins leaped up at once with éclat.

Joy clapped with her family and the rest of the crowd at the end of the show and then left the Whale Arena for the next activity.

As the family moved on, they came to the amusement ride section of the park. There was a ride called *Rio Loco*: Spanish for "Crazy River." *Rio Loco* was a winding waterway with bumps and swells everywhere; these were designed to make big waves! In what looked to be a large inner-tube people could go down *Rio Loco*.

Joy and her family tried *Rio Loco*; they were soon splashed by water thrown up from the bumps. Then, near the end of the ride, as the family rounded a bend (which again sprayed them), they saw a waterfall ahead. Joy thought the waterfall would douse her, but the inner tube kept turning in circles until Mommy and Ethan were right under it! Ethan ducked away and didn't get quite so wet. The water then poured mostly onto Mommy, who had been the driest one in the group...until now!

After leaving *Rio Loco*, the family walked over to their next activity. They soon stood under a huge shape looming over them—a roller coaster. The children asked to be taken on a very hilly roller coaster. Daddy jokingly said it was a great way to dry off after *Rio Loco*. As wet as Mommy was, though, she didn't come with them.

At the roller coaster's landing station, Joy's and Ethan's heights were measured. Fortunately, both were tall enough to ride the coaster. The roller coaster cars were just arriving, and the family made sure to get good seats at the front. Joy sat in the very first car with Daddy, and Ethan sat by himself just behind.

Only a handful of people got onto the roller coaster. After car doors were shut tightly and handlebars locked in place, the train of cars lurched forward. It soon turned and began its ascent.

As the coaster rose over the trees, Joy looked over the park and people milling below. She saw the water of the Whale Arena sparkling in the sun, the *Rio*

Loco's crazy twists and turns, and the winding paths leading to Ocean Park's other attractions.

Joy suddenly remembered she was on a roller coaster and turned around to see the car she was in plunge downward! Joy white-knuckle-gripped her handlebar, and her stomach felt queasy. For a moment, Joy regretted she got on the roller coaster.

Behind Joy, Ethan cowered down as far he could in his seat. Daddy, on the other hand, laughed as if he were on solid ground. Screams and shouts rang out from other people on the coaster.

All this happened in a few seconds! At the bottom of the descent, Joy caught a fleeting glimpse of a camera to the side of the track flashing a picture of her. Up and down the roller coaster went, until it stopped altogether at the station.

Joy got out of her car quite shaken; her heart was nearly pounding out of her chest. Daddy and Ethan, however, looked fine (especially Daddy, who looked *more* than fine).

Later, the family arrived at a Children's Area. It was a huge play fort sitting on a very shallow pool of water. Near the top of the structure was a big bucket that slowly filled with water. When it was full, it tipped over and dumped water onto people standing below.

Joy and Ethan played freeze tag in the shallow pool with other children. They also stood under the bucket of water to have water pour down on top of them. Joy and Ethan spent an hour playing in the Children's Area.

Nearby, the family found another roller coaster, which had a looped and twisted track. Unfortunately, Ethan was too short to go on this ride. Disappointed, he turned and sat with Mommy on a bench close by.

Joy (who, on the other hand, could go on this ride) and Daddy sat down in the first row of the coaster. The seats were hanging down from the track, so Joy and Daddy were basically hanging in midair. They buckled their safety belts before the roller coaster started.

Joy shut her eyes and mouth tightly during the whole ride. Her stomach churned as she hit the loops and turns. The ride seemed longer than it should have been. Only when she sensed the roller coaster stop did Joy unclench her jaw. However, she got off the ride wishing that she had opened her eyes to see the upside-down view.

Joy and her family continued on through the park and came to a large water slide. It had inner tubes that went down big half pipes, and these tubes could fit four people. Joy found the slide rather scenic, especially at the end, when it passed under a clear tunnel that showed a pool above with stingrays in it. The stingrays were the same ones that Joy and Ethan had fed much earlier that day.

The day was drawing to a close. There was an afternoon seal show, which the family decided to watch. Seated inside a semicircle theater, Joy and her family looked toward the stage in front. There was a tank of water, like the one in the Whale Arena, only quite small. On the stage there was a row of entrances in a wall made to look like houses.

After some minutes, five seals, including a baby seal, waddled onto the stage out of an opening and jumped into the pool of water. The seals frolicked with each other until three seal trainers also appeared and opened the show.

The show began with the seals performing typical tricks, such as balancing balls on their noses, but it soon became a comedy, in which the seals acted mischievously. They clapped their flippers, scurried in and out of entrances, and gulped down fish from the trainers' treat buckets—all behind the trainers' backs! The trainers, supposedly becoming exasperated, chased the seals through the entrances and pretended to pass out from fright when a seal barked at them from behind. The show ended with the seals "reviving" their trainers using their version of CPR and being rewarded with fish. Then, the seals and trainers left the stage.

After the seal show ended, the park was about to close. To end the fun day, Daddy took the children on the hilly roller coaster again. Joy braced herself for the roller coaster's drop and did not scream.

On the way out of the park, the family stopped at a souvenir shop to buy a reminder of their day at Ocean Park. Joy chose out a thousand-piece puzzle of dolphins swimming near a reef, Ethan got a bouncy ball, and Mommy chose a magnet to hold up papers on the refrigerator.

Outside, Mommy had Ethan and Joy pose together for a picture in front of a decorative fountain. The picture, taken by the light of the setting sun, turned out to be a great souvenir all on it's own.

Chapter 12

BEGINNING OF JULY

One Saturday morning, Joy and Mommy cleaned the house and cooked two large casseroles and a side of vegetables. Uncle Doug (along with Aunt Kim and Cassie) would arrive in the afternoon and spend time with the family. By 3:00 p.m., everything had been prepared, and Uncle Doug pulled into the driveway.

Daddy, Ethan, and Joy went outside to greet Uncle Doug and his family and welcome them into the house. Mommy encouraged the visitors to sit on the living room couches and make themselves comfortable.

Daddy initiated a conversation, and, before long, talk gravitated to another family outing. Aunt Kim suggested meeting at an amusement park. Uncle Doug, pursuing the idea, mentioned a large arcade he passed every day on his way to work; it was called Austin Arcade. In a few minutes, a plan developed:

next Saturday, both families would spend the entire day at Austin Arcade.

Once the matter had been settled, the adults and children held separate discussions. Joy told Cassie about her experiences at Ocean Park, and Ethan described his latest biplane model. When Cassie indicated she wanted to see Ethan's model, Joy quietly stood at Mommy's side and waited until the conversation subsided. "Mommy, can we go upstairs and show Cassie our projects?" she asked politely.

"Yes, go ahead. I'll let you know when dinner's served."

Joy, Ethan, and Cassie dashed upstairs and crowded into Ethan's closet. Cassie admired Ethan's new model and studied several of his other creations.

Joy showed Cassie a puzzle she had been putting together. It was on a desk in the loft. The puzzle, a picture of exotic animals in a lush jungle, consisted of two thousand pieces. Completion of the puzzle slowed as there were numerous green pieces.

Cassie eagerly offered to help piece together the puzzle. As Cassie, Joy, and Ethan worked together, Joy saw the wide gaps in the picture slowly shrink. The three children were so absorbed in their work they almost didn't realize when Mommy called, "Come and eat!" The children bolted down the steps and rushed to their places at the table.

After dinner, when the table had been cleared, Daddy brought out a pack of cards to play Hearts and Spades. Card games had almost become a tradition, since they brought good memories to Daddy and Uncle Doug. Daddy shuffled the deck and dealt to four players. Since Mommy and Aunt Kim were uninterested in joining the game, they washed the dishes and afterward sat down and talked. Because Daddy and Uncle Doug indisputably played in every round, only two of the children could play at a time. Joy and Cassie agreed to alternate, and Joy persuaded Cassie to go first.

Uproarious laughter rang out as play progressed. Daddy and Uncle Doug cracked jokes back and forth, and the children hooted with glee as they laid trump or a dreaded Queen of Spades. Joy's, Ethan's, and Cassie's eyes shone with anticipation and excitement.

No one noticed three hours had passed. When Ethan happened to glance at the clock between rounds, he exclaimed, "Wow! It's seven o'clock!" Once everyone discerned the lateness of the hour, the game ended. Uncle Doug, Aunt Kim, and Cassie prepared to leave, and Joy and her family went outside with them. As Uncle Doug's car drove away, Cassie rolled down her window and shouted, "Bye! God-willing, we'll see you at Austin Arcade!"

The following Saturday, Joy awakened at 4:30 a.m. She brought a small book bag with things she packed the night prior downstairs for the trip. Joy found Daddy sitting at the table waiting for breakfast. "'Morning, Daddy," Joy said brightly. "'Morning, Mommy!"

Mommy stood beside the stove stirring an omelet.

She gave Joy a hug and continued preparing breakfast. Joy sat down at the table with Daddy, and Ethan appeared in the kitchen just as Mommy served the food. When everyone was seated, the family said grace and began eating. The meal consisted of an *arepa*, a kind of cornbread, topped with melting cheese; a slice of omelet; and hot chocolate.

After breakfast, the family departed. In fifteen minutes, as the sun peeked over the horizon, the Snavely's family vehicle entered the roadway. They had traveled many miles when Uncle Doug called Daddy and said he was approaching Exit 134. Daddy was about two miles behind Uncle Doug, so Uncle Doug slowed until he saw Daddy in his rearview. Both families continued the trip until the GPS' automated voice announced they were nearing their destination— Austin Arcade. Nearing their highway exit, Joy observed an enormous parking lot, a sprawling building, winding go-kart tracks, a small roller coaster, a bright aquamarine pond, and all kinds of kiddie rides. Joy realized that, to enjoy *all* the activities available at this place, they would need at least two days. No wonder it was necessary to arrive at an early hour!

The vehicles soon occupied suitable parking spaces. Everyone exited their cars and walked to the entrance.

The clear sunny morning gave way to the dark interior of the building. The two-story arcade was lit by neon and brightly flashing lights from game booths. Toward the back of the huge room, there were doors that led to all the outdoor fun.

At the front counter, the group's park fees were paid, and a green wrist band was placed on each guest. They then were given a list of activities available at the park. There were so many things to do the children didn't know what they wanted first!

The children chose rock climbing first. Joy fitted herself into her harness. The harness was worn and grimy from constant use, yet Joy fastened the straps and buckles to a comfortable position and grabbed the first handhold of the rock wall. On her way up, Joy noticed Cassie and Ethan were ascending as well. Joy was glad she did not have a fear of heights, since the rock wall was twenty feet high. As Joy scaled the wall, the course became trickier. More than once, Joy retraced her path and got different hand and foot holds. Barely able to stretch her hand high enough, Joy tapped the buzzer at the pinnacle. She looked down over her shoulder: her family looked so small below!

As she descended, Joy saw her brother and Cassie finish their courses. When she touched the floor, Joy removed her harness and went to another section of the rock wall. Joy, Ethan, and Cassie climbed all the courses in the building. Ethan, however, couldn't quite finish one course, most likely because his arms were shorter than the girls'.

The adults bowled with a twelve-pound, dark blue ball. The group set up the game on one lane.

Joy, Cassie, and Ethan each shared a bright orange, nine-pound bowling ball. The adults: the group set up the game on one lane.

When her first turn came, Joy bowled with a dramatic flourish…ending in a gutter ball. After that, Joy dropped more than half the pins on most bowls. There were occasional gutter balls countered by a couple of spares.

Daddy and Ethan dropped pins right and left. They earned first and second place, respectively. When Ethan got two strikes in a row, Joy cheered loudly for her brother.

With bowling out of the way, the group headed outside to the bumper-boating area. Joy's family waited in line for sufficient boats to accommodate them. When at least seven boats were available, Joy and her group secured them.

Joy untied her boat from the quay and maneuvered into the pond. On top of the steering mechanism were buttons, that, when pressed, shot a jet of water in the direction the boat was going.

As boats milled around the pond, like ducks in a puddle, water streamed in every direction. Joy ducked every time she saw water coming her way. Joy managed to spray everyone in her group, and others sprayed her. By the time ten minutes of boating were up and everyone had to moor, Joy was dreached.

Next on the list of activities was mini-golf. At the entrance to the mini-golf course, Joy's group received balls, clubs, and a scorecard with a pencil. There were eighteen holes along the path that traversed the fairways.

Water traps were comprised of artificial ponds, streams, and cascades. Bushes lining the fairway made good places to lose golf balls. The golfing levels were jam-packed with little knolls which required harder hits to get over, rocks which threatened progress, angled edges which changed balls' direction, and tubes that carried the balls to other terraced courses.

Because of these challenges, rarely anyone made par…much less a birdie. There were occasional instances when one member of the group pulled off a terrific shot. For example, Joy was on one of the levels with tubes. She got the ball down the first tube, squarely into the second tube, and into the hole—all in one shot!

Most other courses, however, took many shots to complete. Joy's group finished mini-golf with some higher-end scores (which, of course, weren't commendable).

Revisiting the mini-golf entrance, the group returned their balls and clubs. The group reached the section of the park with kiddie rides, which the children wanted to experience. They rode a small roller coaster, which was nothing compared to the ones in Ocean Park, and a carousel.

Stepping into the carousel, Joy, Ethan, and Cassie got into a round, spinning seat. As the ride got underway, the children began turning the center wheel. Joy felt the speed increasing until it was dizzying. The sights before her were a blur. Joy pulled on the wheel with all her might to keep it going faster. As they spun, the children gave out *whee*s and shouts.

Just as Joy felt lightheaded, the ride ended. Joy got off the carousel. The ground reeled under her as she tried to make a beeline for her family. Joy lurched to the left, then stumbled forward. She grabbed whatever she could for support. Thankfully, Joy's shakiness quickly left her, and she desired to ride the carousel again.

Afterwards came go-karting. There were two tracks. One was relatively simple and easy, while the other track was a Slick Track. The group tried the easy track first.

Beginning of July

Joy sat down in a bright yellow go-kart. She watched as Ethan and Cassie claimed a green and white kart, respectively. Daddy got into a blue kart, and Mommy had a yellow kart like Joy's. Both Uncle Doug and Aunt Kim rode in orange karts. Joy made sure her feet were positioned over the gas and brake pedals so she could be ready for whatever happened. Joy and her group waited until most of the other go-karts filled with people. They were then allowed to go with explicit directions from attendants that go-karts were *not* bumper cars; thus, they were not to be used as such. Joy, so as not to bump into the person in front of her, let him go forward a few feet before she moved. She sped up as she turned onto the track.

Joy weaved in and out of traffic, looking for openings to pass and gain the front of the pack. Despite her careful efforts, Joy did inadvertently touch the bumper of a car a little hard. Not surprisingly, Joy also got bumped from the back and side. Many times, Joy had to jam on the brakes to avoid a fender-bender between herself and an ambitious driver.

Everyone was allowed ten laps around the track. Joy and most of her group finished somewhere in the middle of the pack. Ethan finished second.

The cars and track of the Slick Track, however, had a technology which made certain curves of the track seem as if they had oil spills.

As Joy rounded the first bend, she felt her go-kart skid to the edge of the track. With a thump, Joy's kart hit the orange and white barrier. She started up again, grumbling at the fact that several racers had passed her in the meantime. Long story short, Joy fishtailed into other people and barriers…more than once or twice. She came close to last place.

The final activity of the day was playing in the arcade. The only game that interested Joy and Ethan was a race car game. They sat in the booth and played several races until their arcade tickets ran out. Meanwhile, Cassie won a stuffed animal prize at another booth.

As she left the building, Joy recalled all the fun memories of the day. She hoped to share more time with her uncle and his family soon.

Chapter 13

Days of July

The Fourth of July was a Saturday. In the morning, Daddy took the children out to buy fireworks. They drove down the interstate until they came to a large building with a colorful billboard nearby advertising the sale of fireworks.

Once inside the fireworks store, Joy and Ethan looked over the rows of shelves, trying to find their favorite Fourth of July explosives. In their cart, they put smoke bombs, sparklers, pop-its, and some small tanks that were supposed to be propelled forward by sparks. The tanks and smoke bombs were Ethan's. Daddy selected some big fireworks and firecrackers as well.

The bill for the fireworks turned out to be quite expensive ($500, to be exact), but Daddy didn't seem to mind. He wanted his family to have a memorable Fourth of July. Meanwhile, Mommy had gone to the grocery store to get hotdogs, chips, and juice for the celebration.

Around 4:00 in the afternoon, Joy and her family left for the Tellers' house. It was there that they would shoot off the fireworks and have a small, Independence Day party.

When Joy and her family arrived, the Tellers already had their own fireworks set out on the back porch. Joy and Ethan made several trips back and forth from their family's car to put their fireworks near the others. The Teller's grill had been fired up, and now hotdogs were sizzling on it. While the adults talked, Joy, Ethan, and Elizabeth played Uno on the outdoor table. The food was soon ready. Everyone filled their plates with hotdogs, chips, and slices of Mrs. Teller's delicious apple pie topped with ice cream.

Before long, it was time to light the children's mini fireworks. Elizabeth, Ethan, and Joy lit their sparklers, waved the rods around, and watched the designs the light made in the dark. The children also set off their smoke bombs, and clouds of colors— pink, yellow, and green—filled the air so that it was hard to see.

Ethan lit his tanks with high expectations. Unfortunately, out of the five he had, three turned out to be duds. The other two just gave a pitiful performance: they only rolled forward about an inch or so. Ethan was disappointed that his tanks didn't work the way they should.

Joy, Elizabeth, and Ethan also exploded their pop-its by smashing them down on the concrete patio. By the time the little boxes of pop-its were exhausted, it was almost completely dark—a good time to start firing off the large fireworks.

Everyone set out a lawn chair to be in full view of the anticipated display. Daddy and Mr. Teller arranged the explosives, leaving the biggest and best ones for last. Finally, the fuse of the first firecracker was lit.

"Fire in the hole!" shouted Mr. Teller as he and Daddy backed away. With a whiz, a flaming spark shot up into the sky. It seemed to disappear, but exploded into a dazzle of golden light with a loud pop and a fizz.

Most of the other fireworks took off in much the same way. Some had alternating red and green colors, and some ended in streamers and crackles. There were so many different types of fireworks. The finale was spectacular, and it brought several "Wows!" and applause from the audience. All too soon, the pyrotechnic show concluded.

By the light of several flashlights, the families picked up the debris from the grass. There were many blackened spots in the yard where sparks had fallen. All litter was examined for any glowing ashes and tossed into a big, black plastic bag. When everything had been cleaned up, Joy and her family said goodbye to the Tellers and left for home.

Back in her room, Joy went to her window to watch other people's fireworks displays; she managed to see some final flashes of color on the horizon.

The next Wednesday evening, at STARS class, the girls were invited to share their favorite passage from the Bible. Joy shared what she had discovered in Isaiah 54:11-17. That day, Joy had been flipping through her Bible and found herself in Isaiah. Before, Revelation 21:18-20 had been her favorite passage: she liked that it named all sorts of precious stones in the foundation of the new Jerusalem, such as sapphire, beryl, and amethyst. Isaiah listed some of those gems, but they were used in the houses God would build for a scattered Israel, whom God would protect from its enemies. These promises spoke to Joy, and she wrote the passage down and marked the spot in her Bible. She also told Mommy and Daddy about this passage during devotion that night.

Thursday was a rainy day. Flat gray clouds blanketed the earth to the edge of the sky, and rain came down slowly and steadily. Joy felt she had nothing to do. However, Mommy had a solution for that; she told Joy to clean out her closet. Joy rummaged through boxes and misplaced shoes under the glow of her closet ceiling light. Joy's bed and floor were nearly covered with stuff she had placed on them.

Suddenly, Joy caught sight of something given to her at her graduation party. It was the Pom-Pom Puppy project from the Tellers. Joy took out the box and set it on her desk. She would look at it in a minute. Joy hurriedly shoved her things back into her closet. The job was done half-neatly, but the closet was improved. Once she finished, Joy turned off the light and shut the door.

Joy sat down at her desk and began flipping through the pages of her Pom-Pom Puppy instruction booklet. Joy took out her scissors, ruler, and glue and began working. The basic idea was to make two fluffy balls out of yarn using a guide, and, after gluing the two parts together, shape a head and body.

Joy's first puppy didn't turn out so well. She hadn't tied the yarn ball tight enough, and it fell apart. Joy set the failed project aside and, with a little experience behind her, began working on a second dog. Joy made her new pom-pom puppy look like Skippy. The yarn ball "Skippy" came out very well. Joy showed her work to Mommy, who described it adorable. Mommy even liked the first dog Joy had made and said it could be fixed. While Joy cleaned up the mess on her desk, Mommy pieced together the yarn that had fallen out.

Soon after Joy and Mommy were done, Ethan peered around Joy's door. "Can I play a game with you?" he asked Joy.

"Sure!"

The children ran to the game closet. They picked out *Sorry* and set it up on the carpeted floor of the loft. To make the game more interesting, Joy and Ethan each brought a stuffed animal for players.

Ethan brought Teddy, and Joy chose Quiky-Quacky, her little duck. Naturally, Joy played for herself and Quiky-Quacky; Ethan did the same with Teddy. After a long round of *Sorry*—in which Teddy won—Joy and Ethan withdrew to Ethan's room.

Ethan had a huge bin of random plastic blocks that Mommy had bought at a large garage sale for $20. Interestingly, since there had been a layer of matchbox cars over the blocks, Mommy thought she was getting a container of cars for Ethan. It was quite a surprise for everyone to find the blocks, especially for Ethan, who at the time had only a few sets of blocks.

In his room, Ethan showed Joy his newest block creation from scratch: a white, rather cubic car that almost looked like a stock car. Ethan's car thrilled Joy. She helped him build a garage for it and even began designing a house for the driver of the car, who was supposed to represent Ethan in the block world. Slowly, the block walls began to rise above a rather rickety floor. Joy placed little blocks for tables, desks, and stovetops, and used specialty pieces like trunks, chairs, and doors whenever possible. In fact, finding specialty pieces took longer than the actual building process. After Joy added as much as the little house could hold, Ethan decided it wasn't a good design. They tore the house apart and used some of the materials to build a restaurant and a hospital complete with an ambulance. Joy and Ethan then played out some stories with their creations.

When she finished playing with Ethan, Joy went to her room. She took out her pom-pom Skippy, cuddled him, and sat down with him on her beanbag. Joy took out her book, *Little House on the Prairie*, and read it until Daddy came home from work.

Days of July

Chapter 14

BIRTHDAY

The seventeenth of July was Joy's birthday; that day, Joy woke up, not sure if she felt eleven years old. Before she could move, however, Mommy came into her room with a breakfast tray. Mommy had prepared succulent, buttery scrambled eggs and a stack of golden-brown pancakes. Mommy had also arranged a smiley face on the top pancake with strawberries and blueberries. Near the side of the plate, there was chocolate milk and a little pitcher of maple syrup. Joy sat up in her bed and took the tray from Mommy.

"Thank you, Mommy," Joy gratefully said. She ate her delicious breakfast, then read the Proverbs of the day, Proverbs 17. Verse 17, which spoke on a brother being born for adversity, grabbed Joy's attention. Joy didn't understand that part; sure, she and Ethan bickered some, but he wasn't one to make lots of trouble. Joy would later ask Daddy to clarify the meaning of the verse.

When Joy returned to her room after her shower, she found her bed already made and a card sitting on the comforter. She took the card and admired its design. There were various songbirds sitting on sprigs of apple blossoms. After studying the card's face, Joy flipped it open. The first thing she noticed was a ten and one dollar bill tucked inside. She drew out the money so she could see the message in her card. There was a little poem on one side, and Mommy's handwriting on the other. Joy read her card, put it on her desk, and placed the money inside her pink piggy bank.

About four o'clock in the afternoon, Joy was sent upstairs and told to wait until Mommy called her. Joy immediately guessed that Mommy was preparing her birthday celebration. Half an hour later, the doorbell rang, and in the commotion that followed (mainly because of Skippy), it became evident that Elizabeth and Cassie had arrived.

Finally, Mommy called Joy to come downstairs. Some soft music was playing, and Mommy was setting a charcuterie board on the dining table, which was decorated with balloons, ribbons, and streamers. When all the guests were seated, the crackers, cheese, meats, and fruit were portioned out.

After the snack, a large birthday cake was brought out. It was an ice cream cake, with bright blue icing around the rim and sugar sprinkles all over. Mommy set two big #1 candles and eleven smaller candles in a neat pattern on the cake. Joy smiled as her family and friends sang "Happy Birthday" to her. Joy didn't know whether to sing along or remain silent. After the song ended, Joy blew out the candles in one breath. Everyone clapped as the thin streams of smoke from the candles cleared and Mommy began cutting and serving the cake.

Some colorfully packaged gifts were brought out from behind the sofa. Joy sat on the couch and received the first present from Mommy and Daddy. She gingerly opened the wrapping paper and discovered a beautiful new Bible!

For a long time, Joy had desired a leather-bound, NASB study Bible—like Mommy's and Daddy's. Now, Joy had her very own study Bible. She lovingly stroked the cover; the top half was a rich chocolate brown, and the bottom half was a dusky salmon. Joy hugged her Bible then set it aside reverently in order to open her other presents.

Joy looked over her gifts when she finished opening them. She had a *Twister* game, a gray plush elephant, a silver locket, and a blouse to wear to church, plus more birthday cards from her friends. By now it was 6:00 p.m., and the Tellers and family soon departed.

Amid bills and letters addressed to Mommy and Daddy from the evening mail, there was a pink envelope for Joy from Grandmama and Grandaddy.

After opening the envelope, Joy neatly took out and read her birthday card. When she finished, she called her grandparents to thank them.

Birthday

Devotion was a little late due to the party, but Joy still asked Daddy her question about Proverbs 17. Joy used her new Bible to show Daddy the verse. He responded it may be the way Joy imagined, but more likely it was a brother born to *assist* during one's adversity. The definition made good sense to Joy, and she was thankful for her brother Ethan.

At bedtime, Mommy came into Joy's room to say good night to her. "Thank you for my birthday party, Mommy," Joy said appreciatively. "I had a great time."

"*Me alegro, pequeña mia*," Mommy responded. "I'm glad you liked it."

As a birthday wish, Joy requested Daddy take her to the Lampasas River trails. The next day at six in the morning, Daddy woke Joy by turning on her ceiling light. At the sudden, brilliant glare, Joy squeezed her eyes shut and rolled out of bed. Joy grinned at Daddy and then set some clothes out for the hike.

When Joy and Ethan (Ethan having been awakened in much the same way as Joy) were ready, they went downstairs and glanced hungrily at the breakfast table, which was set with four plates of scrambled eggs and quesadillas.

After eating breakfast, Joy hastily shoved water bottles and snacks into a knapsack. Although she knew Daddy wouldn't leave without her, Joy didn't want to keep him waiting. After saying goodbye to Mommy, Joy and Ethan ran outside and pulled the front door shut.

The family walked down several of their neighborhood's streets to reach the trailhead. They descended into the forested recreational area.

Joy looked up into the flecked green canopy overhead. The drone of cicadas filled Joy's ears. She could smell the earthy scent of decaying leaves on the forest floor. It was warm today, warm even under the trees.

Out of the many trails along the river, Daddy chose one trail leading upstream. Daddy went first, with Joy behind him, and Ethan brought up the rear.

Joy grew accustomed to the rhythmic *tramp-tramp-tramp* of three pairs of feet, the incessant humming of tree-dwelling insects, and the rush of water over rocks in the nearby river.

Once, the three of them came across a fallen oak tree which stretched across the river. Joy, who considered climbing her hobby, went around the uprooted base and pulled herself onto the thick trunk. When she stood up and gained her balance, Joy crossed the river. As the trunk narrowed, branches began shooting up to provide extra stability, but they conversely became smaller. Finally, the limbs became so thin it seemed they would break if Joy stepped on them. By then, Joy could reach the other side of the river with a simple jump, but Joy returned to Daddy and Ethan instead.

As they continued on the trail, Joy saw a pair of deer antlers sticking out from under a mound of leaves. Intrigued, Joy picked up the antlers and realized they were attached to an entire deer skull! Joy examined the skull cautiously; it was a perfect specimen. She looked at the eye sockets, the row of teeth, and the little zigzag lines where the cranium fused together.

Joy showed the skull to Daddy and Ethan. Much as Joy wished to show it to Mommy, she knew she couldn't. Joy set the skull on a rock in a conspicuous place for other passersby to see.

After some time, there appeared to be a small escarpment jutting out parallel to the trail. It had many ledges, clefts, and handholds…perfect for climbing. Joy and Ethan asked to ascend it, and Daddy agreed. He boosted Joy then Ethan onto the first overhang and pulled himself up next.

As they progressed upward, Joy noticed that the rock began opening up into a wedge-shaped cave. There were three "stories" to the cave, with large fissures through which a person could get to the next level.

Joy, aided by Daddy, pushed herself through the openings. At the top, she stepped aside to make room for Ethan when she heard a noise behind her. From the back of the cave, a vague, awkward shape came lumbering forward. Joy screamed. Her mind fraught with fright, Joy thought it was a monkey. Split seconds later, she realized it was a buzzard! It flapped out to the safety of the treetops. Ethan and Daddy asked what had happened; Joy explained.

Afterwards, they began to examine the cave. Names carved into the limestone walls clearly indicated that Joy and her family weren't the first visitors. At the extreme end of the grotto, amid dust and a strong, musty odor, they discovered a sort of alcove. Inside, there were four eggs, undoubtedly belonging to the buzzard that had just flown out.

With the small cave thoroughly explored, the family resumed their climb up the cliff. When they finally reached the top, above the trees by the river and in the bright sunlight, Joy was glad the ascent was over. Now there was just a walk across a field, where the houses of their neighborhood lay beyond.

Joy, weary from the hike, was grateful to see home. Her trudging pace automatically quickened, and in no time, Daddy was unlocking the front door.

At the dinner table that evening, Daddy, Joy, and Ethan told Mommy all about their day. Joy was especially excited to share her incident with the "monkey-buzzard."

Chapter 15

LAST DAYS OF SUMMER

Summer vacation was shortly ending. The majority of Joy's days consisted of helping Mommy with chores, running errands with her, playing with Ethan, and waiting for Daddy to come home from work each weekday.

One day, Mommy took Joy and Ethan grocery shopping. Joy brought along her birthday money to find something on which to spend. Ethan pushed the cart, and Joy helped Mommy put things into the cart. Mommy got fruit and vegetables from the produce section. She even got a strange fruit called a *cherimoya*. It was a tropical South American fruit, with a greenish-brown color; soft, scaly skin; and an upside-down pear shape. Joy held it to her nose; the fruit smelled like a rotten banana. She hoped the *cherimoya* tasted better than it smelled, and Mommy assured her it did.

Last Days of Summer

At the meat section, Joy decided she wanted to buy a piece of steak with her own money. She spent several minutes choosing the biggest, leanest cut of beef she could find. Joy would help Mommy sauté the meat for dinner.

At the checkout line, Joy placed her purchases behind Mommy's so she could pay with her cash. She had gotten apples and her favorite cereal in addition to her meat. Of the $11 she entered the store with, Joy retained 27 cents.

Once home, Joy tossed salad, cooked some rice with black beans, and seasoned the meat. When the meal was ready, Joy was proud to tell Daddy that she had chosen the cut of beef, bought it with her own money, and helped Mommy in the preparation. When

Daddy had eaten, he told Joy the meat was juicy, flavorful, and gristle-free.

After they finished cleaning the kitchen, Mommy gave Joy and Ethan a taste of *cherimoya*. The inside of the fruit was white and pulpy, with large black seeds, and it smelled rotten. Mommy scooped out the pulp with a spoon and gave some to Ethan and Joy.

From the look on Ethan's face, *cherimoya* wasn't good. Nonetheless, Joy thought *cherimoya* the most delicious fruit ever. *Cherimoya* was like a mellow banana, a fragrant apple, and a juicy kiwi all combined. Joy liked it so well she asked Mommy for more, and Mommy ate some as well. They quickly ate the entire *cherimoya*, and Mommy saved the seeds in the hope they might be planted someday.

The time to begin school was at hand. Mommy had already ordered the new school year's books from A Beka, and Joy and Ethan needed to shop for school supplies.

The day of the shopping trip, Joy got in the car and began reviewing her list of things she needed. Throughout the trip to the office supply store, she racked her brains, trying to think of new things to add to her list.

At the store, Joy pulled out her own cart, so as not to confuse her things with Ethan's. After searching through nearly every aisle (to Mommy and Ethan's vexation), Joy collected enough...or more than enough...supplies. In fact, when Mommy checked over Joy's cart, she found some unnecessary or duplicate items.

Joy was unhappy Mommy wanted her to return some things. Joy had all her new school supplies picked out to match perfectly, but now she would have to use items from last year. Joy grumbled as she took glittery clipboards and pencil pouches out of her cart.

Suddenly, Joy realized she had no right to complain about not getting everything she wanted. Mommy was kind enough to let Joy get new things for her school year, but Joy was making a fuss for things she probably wouldn't use anyway! *("God, forgive me for being greedy and having an attitude when I didn't get what I wanted. Help me show gratitude for what I have.")*

When the cut had been made, Joy counted her things: packs of pencils, colored pens, and highlighters; notebooks; a pink binder; loose-leaf notebook paper; and a calendar.

Upon arriving home, Joy took her school supplies to her room. She still felt badly about her attitude, and rather listlessly began placing notebooks into her desk drawers and pens, pencils, and highlighters into some jars.

As Joy arranged her things, Mommy came into Joy's room carrying a pink, flowery clipboard. Mommy handed it to Joy and said, "I know you wanted a clipboard, and I only used this one a few times. I told you not to get a new clipboard at the store because I already had one."

"Thank you, Mommy," Joy said. "I realize that it would have been a waste of money to buy everything new for me. I apologize for being upset when you told me to put some things back. Could you please forgive me?"

Mommy forgave Joy, and Joy felt much better after she restored her relationship with God and Mommy. Once she finished organizing everything, Joy looked at her room in satisfaction; finally, everything was ready for the new school year.

A couple of days later, Joy's and Ethan's A Beka books and DVDs arrived in the mail. As a team, Joy and Ethan brought the heavy packages into the house and carried them to the loft. New schoolbooks were almost as exciting as Christmas presents! Mommy lent Ethan a box cutter, which he used to slice open the box flaps.

Joy and Ethan removed plastic wrappings and set to work sorting out their books, since they came jumbled. Using the invoice, Joy and Ethan knew which books were theirs and which books were for Mommy (the home-teacher grading books). Meanwhile, Skippy sniffed all around the boxes and tried to chew on the wrapping. Joy and Ethan quickly removed the temptation.

When they had finished, Joy and Ethan sneak-peeked into their new books. They flipped through math and English workbooks and read snippets of history and science textbooks.

Joy looked over her sixth-grade books. They were similar to last year's, only less colorful and more difficult. Joy's grammar book also outlined a few book reports for her to do; there was also a Library Research Report, a formidable assignment for someone who had never written one before. Joy realized that this school year was going to bring new challenges, but would also be fun and exciting.

Chapter 16

A FINAL ADVENTURE

A special event was planned to celebrate the end of summer on the second-to-last Saturday before school. The Snavely family agreed a few hours playing in the Lampasas River would be suitable recreation. They also invited the Tellers and Uncle Doug, Aunt Kim, and Cassie to be with them at the Lampasas River.

Toward afternoon, Daddy drove his family down to the gravel parking lot beside the river. They brought a packed lunch basket, swim gear, and Skippy.

The first thing the family did was set up their picnic on one of the tables in a pavilion. The invitees arrived, and, with extra sides such as cookies and chips provided by the guests, the families enjoyed a meal of sandwiches and fruit.

After cleaning leftovers and throwing away garbage, the families looked at a map of the trails. The map was an old signboard with a yellowed plastic covering and half-rotted wood. While the adults chose the trail to take, Ethan, Joy, and her friends observed the cobwebs, spiders, and egg sacs in the nooks and crannies. Ethan pointed out the spiders and explained them to the girls. Joy shivered and kept her distance, but Cassie seemed quite interested in Ethan's explanation.

The small hike lasted only a half-hour. After returning to the pavilion, the children prepared to swim.

There had been a recent rain, the river had a stronger current than usual; therefore, the children were told to play near the bank.

A Final Adventure

When some minutes of playing passed, Joy waded a little farther upstream to where a large rock jutted out of the bank. Joy climbed onto the rock and leaped into the water. She had angled the jump so that she wouldn't land in the shallows or the deep current.

After a few more jumps, Joy overreached her bounds. In showing off to the other children, she landed in the dreaded current. Swiftly and silently, it carried Joy past the bank where her family stood.

The water got deeper and deeper. Joy stretched her legs and feet and tried to touch the bottom, but she barely reached the gravel of the riverbed. Joy began to panic when Mommy, who had finally realized what was going on, shouted, "Joy!"

The way Mommy said it chilled Joy. In a blind effort, she went underwater and attempted to swim directly against the current. When Joy came up, she was farther than ever from her family.

Mercifully, Elizabeth's mom had once been a lifeguard at the local swimming pool. Mrs. Teller remembered her training from college and put it into practice to save Joy.

Mrs. Teller swam speedily to Joy, caught her under the arms, and struck out for the nearest bank. Mrs. Teller used a tree branch projecting over the river to climb onto shore, where they rejoined Joy's family.

The embarrassment Joy experienced a few minutes later was dreadful. She could hardly face her family and friends. Later, Joy got enough resolve to share her story.

After the Tellers and Uncle Doug and his family left, Joy and her family returned home. Daddy surprised Joy by telling her to get a piece of paper and pen. Joy nervously expected a lecture, but Daddy instructed her on how to get out if she ever found herself in a river current again. Joy wrote down what Daddy said.

First, Daddy told Joy to swim *with* the current and angle herself toward the nearest bank. Next, he said to jump as the riverbed grew shallower and keep going until solid ground was reached.

"Those are good instructions," thought Joy. *"But hopefully I'll never have to use them."*

Next Sunday, at church, Pastor Kearney had a guest speaker from Israel; his name was Rabbi Davies. Rabbi Davies spoke on the unity of believers and how his life's mission, bringing Jews to Christ, played a part in that coherence. At the end of his sermon, he gave the congregation a challenge: fast each morning for a week while praying for the Peace of Jerusalem and for the spreading of the gospel.

After the closing remarks and prayer, everyone went to the foyer of the church where Rabbi Davies had arranged some tables. He had brought articles from his country, such as flags, prayer shawls, small flasks of anointing oil, and trinkets carved from special materials found in Israel. Some things were for display only, others were for sale.

Daddy bought Mommy, Joy, and Ethan some things from Rabbi Davies's tables. Joy picked out a necklace with a garnet-like Star of David pendant. Ethan got a shofar, though his ram's horn was rather short compared to other shofars Rabbi Davies displayed. Mommy chose a little bottle of anointing oil, made of frankincense and olives.

When Joy and Ethan brought their things home, they tried them out. Joy wore her necklace the rest of the day, and Ethan blew on his shofar. Instead of sounding a long trumpet blast, Ethan made buzzing and squeaking noises. After many attempts, Ethan learned how to play it by vibrating his lips. Skippy ran to Ethan every time he heard the shofar, thinking it was a chew toy for him. Skippy even swiped the shofar one time when Ethan set it on the sofa within Skippy's reach.

Mommy, Joy, and Ethan implemented Rabbi Davies's challenge to fast and pray half a day. The next day around sunrise, Joy and Ethan got up with Mommy and knelt on the living room rug to pray. Daddy was away at work, so he couldn't pray with his family. Joy, Ethan, and Mommy prayed for about an hour. Afterwards, Joy and Ethan read their Bibles. When they finished, Joy and Ethan played quietly or read other books, but sporadically they prayed with Mommy.

Joy was very hungry early in the morning while she was fasting, but the hunger gradually diminished, although her stomach rumbled often. She was glad when, after noon, she could eat a parfait of yogurt, granola, and fruit.

For a whole week the family fasted and prayed in the morning, then resumed the normal schedule.

Nevertheless, whenever Joy saw her necklace, she prayed more frequently.

The next Sunday evening, Joy set out her schoolbooks and reread the materials she needed to know. She sharpened her pencils and organized her notebooks, textbooks, and DVDs in neat stacks.

Joy went downstairs to the kitchen, where she helped Mommy fill the Crock Pot with steak, potatoes, green beans, baby carrots, and water. By lunchtime the next day, God-willing, it would be a delicious stew.

Joy set her alarm for 5:00 a.m. She pulled back the covers of her bed and settled into her blankets, hugging her plush toys tightly.

Joy made sure to end her day with God. She talked to Him the same way would talk to a friend, only this Friend knew and supplied everything. First, Joy thanked God for her new school year. Then she prayed for her family and Cassie and Elizabeth and their families. Joy told God her fears, hopes, thoughts, and feelings. She ended her prayer and fell asleep.

Just as the sun peaked over the horizon the next morning, Joy began dreaming she was standing in a town square with her family. There was a clock tower at one end of the square, and it began to ring with deep tones. Soon, however, it changed to a high-pitched, rapid ringing—Joy's alarm clock!

Joy awakened with a start and switched off her clock before it rang any more. She sat laughing about her dream and thought it should be shared with someone… Joy suddenly realized with a shiver down her spine it was the first day of school. She had forgotten during the night.

Joy had mixed feelings toward school. The long-expected school year would commence today, but Joy dreaded it in some ways. She was relieved the first few days would be fairly easy until Joy could resume the routine of school

Then, the delightful smell of cooking stew wafted up to Joy; just the aroma calmed her. Joy anticipated spooning the broth later that day.

After reading a chapter or two of her Bible, Joy made her bed and smoothed every crease from her comforter. She plumped up the pillows and set them in their positions. Lastly, Joy took her plush toys and placed them carefully in front of the pillows.

Joy went over to her desk chair, where some clothes hung over its back. Joy's new outfit consisted of new navy-blue shorts and a green top.

Everyone else was awake by this time. Daddy went to work, Mommy would cook breakfast, and Joy and Ethan launched into school.

Joy and Ethan went upstairs to their schoolrooms, which was the loft for Joy and the upstairs studio for Ethan. Mommy came upstairs to pray that Joy and Ethan would have wisdom and diligence to complete their year with excellence.

After the prayer, Joy sat down at her desk and inserted the first disk, Bible class, into the desktop computer drive. She waited for the menu to appear on the screen, then hit play...

About
Kharis Publishing:

Kharis Publishing, an imprint of Kharis Media LLC, is a leading Christian and inspirational book publisher based in Aurora, Chicago metropolitan area, Illinois. Kharis' dual mission is to give voice to under-represented writers (including women and first-time authors) and equip orphans in developing countries with literacy tools. That is why, for each book sold, the publisher channels some of the proceeds into providing books and computers for orphanages in developing countries so that these kids may learn to read, dream, and grow. For a limited time, Kharis Publishing is accepting unsolicited queries for nonfiction (Christian, self-help, memoirs, business, health and wellness) from qualified leaders, professionals, pastors, and ministers. Learn more at: https://kharispublishing.com/